Mystery at Black Point

Mystery at Black Point

Kristoffer E. Johnson

Lighthouse
eBooks

I dedicate this book to my mother Cleon Johnson who passed away from cancer in 1987. I want to thank her for the spiritual investment she made in my life.

Mystery at Black Point is the second book in the Eagle Chronicle series. The first book, *The Renegade's Wine*, is also by Kristoffer E. Johnson.

Mystery at Black Point

Copyright © Kristoffer E. Johnson 2005
This revised edition © 2008

This book is a work of fiction. Named locations are used fictitiously, and characters and incidents are the product of the author's imagination. Any resemblance to actual events or places or persons, living or dead, is entirely coincidental.

Published by
Lighthouse Christian Publishing
SAN 257-4330
5531 Dufferin Drive
Savage, Minnesota, 55378
United States of America

www.lighthouseebooks.com
www.lighthousechristianpublishing.com

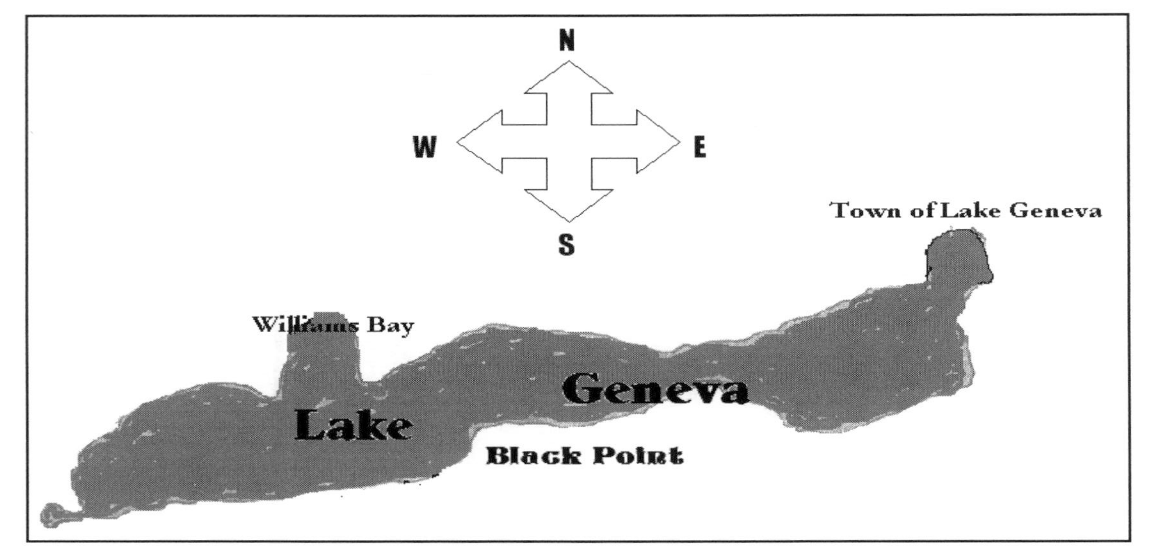

N
W
E
S
Town of Lake Geneva
Williams Bay
Lake
Geneva
Black Point

CHAPTER ONE

It was 1988 and the shores of Lake Geneva, Wisconsin were bustling with the signs of a new summer. Freshly painted piers reflected the warm sun, and the nearby storefront windows displayed the latest swim-wear and beach accessories for the Chicago tourists.

John Benedict slowly exited his Lincoln with a large stack of papers in his right hand, carefully balancing a cup of hot coffee in his left. He nudged the car's heavy door with his shoe and made the trek to his real estate office where he opened the office door and dropped the papers onto his desk. While sighing in relief he noticed the answering machine had some messages. He pressed the start button, and eased his body into the warm leather chair. The machine finished rewinding and he was ready with pen and paper.

"Hi, John, I'm calling about the condo in Cedar Crest. I'd appreciate a call at . . ."

John quickly forwarded the message knowing the condo had already sold nearly a week ago.

"Well, message two," he murmured to himself.

"Hi, my name is Cameron Fossberg, and I'm calling about the estate currently for sale on Black Point. My wife and I are planning to come up this weekend and stay at my parents' summer home. I was wondering if you could give me a call at their number sometime on Saturday morning. The number is 765-0987."

John frowned as he listened to the message one more time while writing every detail of the recorded voice. Then he picked up the phone and dialed the number. "Yes, may I speak to Cameron Fossberg? Thanks. This is John Benedict with Benedict Realty. I'm returning his call. Sure, I'll hold."

There was a brief pause. "Mr. Fossberg, this is John Benedict. You called me about the Black Point property."

He listened intently as the voice on the other end responded.

"What time did you say, Mr. Fossberg? Ten A.M.

this morning at the property? Hold on, let me look at my calendar and see if I've any other commitments." John paged through the thick leather planner to the current date. "No, that time slot is fine. I'll meet you there. Thanks."

Click.

John sat back in his chair, deep in thought as he chewed on his pen. It was extremely rare to get any calls on this property. The picture of it in the real estate magazine made the house come across like a palace, but when prospective buyers saw it first hand, they backed out immediately. It was also a very difficult property to get to unless you knew the narrow streets of the south shore. He shrugged. Since Cameron Fossberg seemed to know where the property was, he had almost certainly seen it. Something didn't seem to add up.

John steered his silver Lincoln slowly through the gated entrance at around 9:30 A.M. He wanted to get there a little early to see if anyone else might be showing it, however doubtful that would be. As he drove along the grass-laden cobblestone driveway, John noticed a late model BMW parked under the large carport attached to the east side of the house. The Illinois plates said "HAMMER."

He parked behind the BMW and quickly exited the Lincoln, hoping the prospective client hadn't been waiting too long. But as he walked along the sports car, he could still hear its exhaust pipes ticking. Whoever was here couldn't have arrived very long ago. A faint conversation grew louder from behind the carport as a young couple rounded the corner of the house. John smiled and quickly approached them. "You must be the Fossbergs."

They were in their early thirties with the appearance of a high society Chicago couple. They both wore his-and-hers stainless steel Rolex watches and summer outfits to match the feeling of wealth that was clearly emulated by their mere existence.

The man smiled. "Yes, I'm Cameron, and this is my wife Morgan."

John returned the smile. "I'm very pleased to meet you. Hope you haven't been waiting long."

Cameron smiled. "No, we only got here five minutes ago. I just wanted to show Morgan around the place. I used to help take care of this property when I was a kid. I was kind of an assistant to the caretaker when the Kholton family owned it."

John listened intently. "That's a name I haven't heard in a long time. So, I'm assuming it's fair to say you know the property better than just about anyone?"

Cameron smirked a little. "I guess you could say that."

"Well, how about a look inside?" John said, with a laugh.

"Great!" both Cameron and Morgan said at the same time.

The large oak doors opened, after a small fight, and the decaying splendor of the house mesmerized John and the Fossbergs. John looked at the woodwork. "I think it goes without saying that they don't make them like this anymore."

The Fossbergs nodded in agreement.

John examined the far reaches of the hallway that were almost lost in the gloom, and wrinkled up his nose in disgust. "Unfortunately, many turn-of-the-century lake homes are being bought just for the property, to build new ones in their place. It's sad to say, but this has been a growing trend for the last fifteen years. I know some people call it progress, but I don't like to see the character of the lake being changed. The history of Lake Geneva is steeped in the architecture that once graced its shores."

Cameron was looking at John while he spoke.

"You're absolutely right, Mr. Benedict. My dad and I were just talking about the old homes this morning over breakfast. That is why I'm suddenly interested in the house."

"Call me John." He started to lead them down the main hallway to the living room. "There has been some talk of tearing this house down for a subdivision, or condos. Did you know that?"

Cameron shook his head. "Perhaps it's fate that I have an interest in this property."

John smiled sheepishly. "Perhaps."

As John slowly made the tour up to the third story, he looked at Cameron and decided to pose a question. "Cameron, I should know my way around this house, but I plead for your forgiveness as I ask this. Do you remember which room has the entrance to the tower?"

Cameron laughed. "Sure. It's the second guest bedroom on the right."

John entered the bedroom first and noticed the unusual door leading to the tower staircase. It was set at a strange angle in the room. He opened it to be greeted by a blanket of cobwebs and dead leaves. The tower was an engineering marvel with a staircase that was severely spiraled, and a hand railing that was custom made to meet the tight specifications of the structure. The Victorian-styled tower clung to the top of the house like a jeweled crown.

John went first, with the Fossbergs following closely behind. The view from the top was absolutely breathtaking as the cool breeze hit his face with full force while he gazed at the shimmering water of Lake Geneva. The Fossbergs stood hand in hand, obviously enjoying the view.

"This is absolutely gorgeous," Morgan said, with a touch of awe in her voice.

Cameron made his way to the edge of the tower and pointed his finger towards the dense forest along the rocky shore of the estate. The trees towered over the lake path like a scene from some mythical fairy tale. "See all those trees? Each one is a different species from all over the world. I remember when I was cutting the grass as a kid, the wind would whistle through the pine needles so loudly that it drowned out the tractor engine."

John made eye contact with Cameron as he listened. "You sure know your stuff about this estate."

Cameron laughed briefly as he led the way back down the staircase. "I always knew that one day I'd own this place."

John's eyebrows rose for a brief moment. "How interested are you in this property, Mr. Fossberg?"

Cameron closed the door to the tower. "Very."

John felt his lips tighten. This sale would be huge, even though he would have to share the commission with another broker. But his heart was convicted to be totally up-front about the decayed state of the property. "I want to be very honest with you, Cameron. I'm a businessman and would very much like to sell you this house, but please understand that it needs a lot of work. To make this place look the way it once did would probably take more than the house is actually worth. The primary value of this property is held in the lake-front acreage. I certainly want the sale, but I also don't want to see a nice young couple make a mistake."

Cameron smiled. "I appreciate the courage it took for you to say that, John, but we really want this house."

John's stomach seemed to be tying itself in knots. God seemed to be giving him a blessing that totally exceeded his expectations. "Mr. Fossberg, may I ask what you do for a living?"

"Sure, I'm a general contractor from Deerfield, Illinois. One of my specialties is restoring old homes."

John felt a little more relieved to know that Cameron understood what he was getting into. "Would you like to come to my office and we can draw up an offer?"

Cameron took out his car keys. "We'll follow you."

*

John was a little late coming home that afternoon as he pondered the events of the day. He was anxious to tell his wife about the Fossbergs and the old Kholton estate. He opened the kitchen door and noticed a note lying on the kitchen counter.

I'm picking up Molly at soccer practice. Will be back in a few minutes.

John smiled and put his briefcase under the table as the door opened, and his wife and daughter came in talking. "Hey, guys, I'm in the kitchen," he called with excitement.

His daughter Molly, and his wife Lynn entered the kitchen and both gave him a big hug. Molly immediately went to the fridge, while Lynn sat at the table to take off her shoes. "You guys will never guess what happened at work today."

Molly and Lynn continued with their current tasks as John was about the spill the news.

"I sold the Kholton estate on Black Point."

Molly closed the fridge door with a plate in her hand and walked to the family room while Lynn slowly looked at John. "You're kidding? Right?"

John started to comb his fingers through Lynn's hair. "I'm serious. I sold the Kholton estate."

Lynn's face burst into the biggest smile. "John, that's unbelievable. But how?"

"A young couple from Chicago came to look at it this morning. The husband's parents have had a summer place in Williams Bay since the late fifties. While growing up here during the summers, he helped the caretaker when the Kholton family owned the property."

"The commission on that place has to be astronomical," Lynn said with excitement.

"I'll have to split it of course with the broker in Geneva, but my share before taxes will be about $75,000."

Lynn acted as though she was beside herself. "I know we've been praying for God's blessing on the business, John, but this is a miracle."

John gave his wife another hug as she stood up from the chair. "That's exactly what I was thinking today as I showed the property. This is God's doing, pure and simple."

*

Later that night the Benedicts' station wagon entered the Grace Community Church parking lot for Wednesday night prayer meeting. Molly crawled out of the back seat and waved to her parents. "I'll see you guys after youth group," she shouted, as she took off towards a group of high school kids near the entrance of the church.

John and Lynn waved goodbye as they made their way across the pavement. Pastor Phil Morse greeted them as they entered the church. "I see they let anyone in here," he joked, as he shook both their hands. "John, I wanted to let you know that the elder board meeting this Sunday is being moved to Monday night at seven. Will that work out for you?"

John smiled. "Shouldn't be a problem."

He walked with Lynn into the sanctuary and sat down in the middle section.

Lynn took his hand and rubbed his fingers. "That sale puts us even closer to our retirement goals."

John put his Bible down and kissed her on the forehead. "God is definitely working. There's no doubt about it."

*

Several weeks had passed since the successful sale of the Kholton estate. John was working on some paperwork one morning when the small bell on the top of the office door-frame jingled, and Cameron Fossberg entered the room.

John rose from his seat and shook Cameron's hand with a firm grip. "Mr. Fossberg, I was just thinking about you. How is the house coming?"

"Well, the progress is slow, but it's shaping up."

"What can I do for you?" John asked.

"Well, I was wondering if you knew when the deed would be ready. I know realtors don't handle that sort of thing, but you seemed to know the title company owner pretty well when we closed on the house, and I've had trouble getting a hold of him."

John had a puzzled look on his face. "Let me give Carl a call and see what's holding things up. I'm sure there's a good explanation for the delay. He really knows his stuff and is pretty efficient as well."

"I'd greatly appreciate it. We don't have phone service yet and all my time has been spent on the house. Any help you can offer would be greatly appreciated."

John shook Cameron's hand a second time. "No problem."

*

John stopped by home for some lunch and was greeted by his daughter Molly in the kitchen. “Hey, kiddo, what’s going on?”

“Well, Dad, I’m trying to find a summer job in the paper and there isn’t much to choose from. I might have to stick with house cleaning and baby sitting again this summer.”

“That’s not the worst. You sure made a killing last year.”

Molly closed the last page of the paper. “I know, I just wanted to do something a little different.”

As John made a sandwich he looked at Molly’s disappointed face. “Do you want to go with me for a little ride to Black Point? I need to drop off some papers.”

Molly wore a weak smile. “Sure, why not.”

*

The trees along Black Point were dense with leaves as John’s Lincoln made the long journey to the main house. He could see scaffolding and piles of unwrapped shingles lining the edges of the exposed foundation. The house looked like it had been through a tornado as large pieces of old wood hung from the corners of the massive Victorian dwelling.

Cameron came out of the house and must have noticed a car coming from the distance. He clearly recognized the Lincoln and started to walk towards the car as it approached the carport.

John walked towards Cameron with a thick stack of papers in a protective plastic folder. “I got a hold of Carl and he had the papers done a few days ago. I apologize for the delay. Like I said before, he’s usually very prompt.”

Cameron smiled and took the papers. “Thank you so much for your help, John.” He noticed Molly sitting in the front seat. “Who is that with you?”

John looked at the car. “Oh, that’s my daughter Molly. She’s a little discouraged right now trying to find a summer job. I thought I’d bring her out with me for a drive.”

Cameron scratched his chin and looked at Molly again through the tinted windshield. “Is that so? Do you think she’d be willing to do some work around here?”

“What did you have in mind?” John asked with curiosity.

“Do you think she’d be willing to help us clean the inside?”

John looked back at Molly and motioned for her

to join the conversation. She exited the car and ran over to her dad and Cameron. "Molly, this is Mr. Fossberg."

Molly pulled her long red hair from her eyes and shook Cameron's hand. "Pleased to meet you."

"Molly, Mr. Fossberg has a business proposition for you."

"Do you think you would want to spend the summer helping my wife and me clean the house? There's more work to last well beyond the summer, and I'll pay you handsomely for your services."

John smiled at Molly. "The decision is entirely yours, kiddo."

She looked at the house for a moment and then at Cameron. "When do you want me to start?"

Cameron smiled, "How about tomorrow morning at eight?" He shook Molly's hand.

"It's a deal," she said solemnly.

CHAPTER TWO

John made sure to have Molly at the estate at eight sharp the next morning. She kissed him goodbye and grabbed the brown bag lunch on the car floor. "I'll see you around three-thirty. Okay?"

"Sounds good," John replied, as she opened the car door.

John watched from the car as Cameron greeted Molly at the back door of the house. He smiled and waved at John as he let Molly in. John put the Lincoln into drive and slowly rolled down the narrow driveway.

Cameron gave Molly a tour of the upper level while pointing out all of the areas that needed to be cleaned. The walls were adorned with dark oak moldings, and the ceilings were shedding plaster pieces like a January snowstorm. Huge sections of torn wallpaper hung from the main hallway as the years of neglect took its toll on the once glorious house. "I'd like to start removing the wall paper from the hallway. Have you ever used a steam remover?"

"I'm not sure," she replied.

Cameron picked up the end of an unusual stainless steel contraption that was lying on the hallway floor. "This device is actually fun to use."

He turned the machine on and in a matter of minutes the large vacuum cleaner-like appendage started to blow out billows of steam. "Just press the end of the steam hose on the paper and it will come right off."

Molly was skeptical at first, but with a few strokes the paper started to peel away. Cameron handed her the end of the machine. "Do you feel up to the job?" he asked, while pointing down the seemingly endless hallway.

Molly nodded. "I think so."

"Do you mind being alone for a while? My wife and I need to go the hardware store for a few things. We shouldn't be gone for more than a couple of hours. Are you comfortable with that?"

Molly shrugged her shoulders. "That's fine. I don't mind being alone."

"I'll turn the radio on to keep you company," Cameron shouted as he wandered down the hallway towards the staircase. See you a little later."

"Sounds good," Molly replied, as she looked down the hallway towards Cameron. She could hear a radio go on with some easy listening rock music. She directed the steam towards the wallpaper as she pondered the massive project. This wasn't exactly what she had in mind for a summer job, but considering what they agreed to pay, she couldn't pass up the opportunity.

About a half-hour went by and Molly was just getting used to the steamer. She was singing to a familiar song on the radio when the nozzle completely stopped in a groove on the wall. She put the nozzle down and took a closer look as the steamer bellowed on the floor. It was different than a chipped piece of drywall; it appeared to have a pattern of some sort, almost like a wood molding. Molly picked up the steamer nozzle and started to work once again on the paper. The paper came off with relative ease as she became more efficient, and soon she had an entire section of the hallway almost completed. She took a moment to stand back and look at her work when something caught here eye. There was a very faint outline that stood in the middle of the hallway. Part of the outline was where the nozzle got caught on the wall, but most of it went far beyond the small groove. She took a few more steps back and tried to view the area with the assistance of some sunlight. She scratched at the groove with her fingernail as the moldy drywall cracked off. Her fingernail dug deep into the damp wall as she pulled her finger back to remove the crusty material. She looked down the hallway to see if anyone was watching. There was something overpowering about the strange outline. It was almost as if a voice was calling her from behind the wall.

"Maybe just one more small piece and then I can see what's behind there," she murmured to herself. She could now fit three fingers into the slot. The damp drywall crumbled all over her hand as she pulled the slimy material back. The corner of a door was now completely visible, and Molly could sense something wasn't right as her heart began to pound. She could now fit all five fingers in the hole as she gripped the filthy material with both hands. A massive piece of drywall came crashing down on the floor and a blinding envelope of dust engulfed the corner of the hallway.

Molly started to cough as the dust began to settle on her body. She was obsessed to see what was behind the door. The pieces became bigger and bigger as her persistence finally revealed three-quarters of the door. She grabbed the doorknob and it slowly opened with a loud rusted shriek. She climbed over the remaining scraps of drywall and opened the badly damaged door.

The room was dark, with a smell like rotting flesh. She could make out some kind of patterns on the walls, but the room was so dark that it was impossible to decipher what they were. She remembered seeing a flashlight on top of a toolbox near the staircase, so she ran down the hallway and grabbed hold of it.

She re-entered the room and fell on the floor as her shoelace caught a jagged piece of drywall. She turned on the light as she lay on the floor and screamed with horror. Her eyes were fixed on the drawings and images that draped the wall from top to bottom. There were drawings of demons and skulls in the middle of the wall, and the tops of the walls were covered with strange symbols and ancient writings.

Molly leaned back on a sharp object that felt like a knife. She shined the light behind her and discovered the floor was littered with candles, matches and rusty knives. The smell was becoming even worse as she wandered towards a large pile of rags in the distance.

She pulled the rags back and her mouth dropped with disbelief as she stared at the dead carcasses of cats and dogs piled neatly under a heavy blanket. The blood was still fresh, which meant someone had been there recently. She crawled out of the room and leaned against the hallway wall breathing erratically as she tried to contain the horror, her body trembling in a seizure-like motion as she began to hyperventilate.

A long shadow moved towards her from the staircase. “Molly,” a voice said from a distance as the vibrations of heavy footsteps rippled through the floorboards.

She tried to move but her uncontrollable breathing paralyzed her body.

“Molly,” the voice said again, as the shadow grew larger and larger from the dark hallway. A hand rested on her shoulder and she passed out.

*

Molly’s eyes opened slowly as her dad and two paramedics greeted her. Cameron and Morgan stood back in disbelief as a policeman asked them questions about the house.

“She’s coming to,” John said with relief as they all

gathered around her.

Molly looked towards the doorway and noticed several policemen dragging plastic bags from the room. She looked at her dad and began to cry. “I’m sorry, Dad, I shouldn’t have gone in there.”

Cameron knelt down and put his hand on her shoulder. “I’m so sorry about this, Molly. I had no idea that room was there.”

The paramedics lifted the stretcher. “We need to take her to the hospital to make sure everything is okay,” one of the paramedics said as he checked the straps.

John had some tears in his eyes. “Cameron, are you sure you don’t know how this stuff got here?”

They both entered the room as the police continued to gather the carcasses.

Cameron shook his head. “John, I’ve no idea what this is.” He walked back to the door and looked at the drywall. “Obviously Molly must have come across this room when she was tearing down the old wallpaper.” He motioned for John to come over by the door. “Look at this. Old homes like this used plaster for walls, but this was made of drywall. Even though it’s damp, whoever sealed this up probably did it within the last ten to fifteen years.”

John went back to the middle of the room and looked at all the drawings and markings on the wall. "I've never seen anything like this before. I don't know how to describe it, but something feels very oppressive in the room. How could someone get in here if that door was sealed?"

Cameron looked at John. "You know, that's a good question. I really wasn't thinking about that, but now that you mention it. . ." He shook his head. "I really don't know." He paced the floor to look for any loose boards, but none could be found.

A policeman walked into the room and headed towards Cameron. "Mr. Fossberg, we're certainly not charging you with anything, but we need to seal this room off with yellow tape. I'm sorry to delay your remodeling project, but one of the county detectives will be here tomorrow to look over the scene."

"John, I can't apologize enough for what happened this afternoon," Cameron said with a sober tone, as he walked with John down the staircase. "Can we visit Molly tomorrow and see how she's doing?"

John was appreciative of his concern. "Let me see, and I'll give you a call."

Cameron shook his hand. "I understand."

John looked back at Cameron as he opened the

back door to the house. "Are you and your wife staying here tonight?"

Cameron stopped to answer. "Morgan is pretty shook up. I think we're going to stay at my parent's home until we can get this thing squared away."

John smiled. "That sounds like a good idea." He closed the door and turned the ignition as he sat deep in thought.

*

John entered the emergency room entrance to Lakeland Hospital and saw his wife Lynn crying in the waiting area. She looked up and saw him walking towards her. "John, what happened in that house?"

John could feel her body trembling as the warm tears soaked through the shoulder of his dress shirt. "Honey, I don't know. I really don't know."

A doctor came out of the emergency room with a smile on his face. "Molly should be all right. We needed to give her a few stitches on her right hand, and a tetanus shot, but other than that you can take her home." He handed John a prescription slip. "This is for a mild sedative so your daughter can relax. Can I ask what happened to her?"

John took the prescription slip. "Let's just say she's had a traumatic day, and leave it at that."

The doctor smiled. “I understand. You have an awfully shaken up daughter in there.”

Lynn’s crying became louder from the doctor’s reply. John put his arm around her shoulder and followed the doctor into the emergency room.

Molly looked up as tears began to fall from her cheek. “I’m so glad to see you.”

John gazed at the floor as he felt his family tremble under his arms. “Let’s go home,” he said with a loving voice.

Lynn and Molly nodded in agreement.

CHAPTER THREE

Dark rain clouds appeared in the western sky as two county squad cars traveled up the long driveway of the Kholton estate the next morning. Cameron Fossberg watched from the kitchen window as the spotless cruisers parked under the massive carport. Two uniformed policemen and one detective wearing a badge over his suit coat lapel exited the cars. Cameron promptly walked out and greeted them as they approached the house.

The detective extended his hand to Cameron. "Mr. Fossberg, my name is Detective Frank Logan."

Cameron shook his hand while the detective pointed at the two uniformed policemen. "These are officers Williams and Grant. They'll be helping me with the investigation." Logan handed Cameron a packet of paper work. "I'll need to you to sign a few things before we can look over the house. Do you have a problem if we do this?"

Cameron quickly consented and the four men entered the kitchen. The massive hallway had remained untouched since the occurrence. The four men stopped in front of the gaping hole, the yellow police tape clashing with the color of the damp drywall. Logan ripped the tape off and entered the room. The spotlights were still in place from the day before and nothing had been touched. He turned on the lights as the two policemen searched the room.

Logan carefully studied each drawing wall by wall and then took a picture of the four sides for his records. Some of the markings he recognized as gang symbols, but some were a complete mystery. "How did anyone get in this room if the only realistic entrance had been sealed off for nearly twenty years?" he whispered to himself.

There were no bookshelves or closet doors, and the only other known exit was a very small oval window that overlooked the front portion of the house. Even a child's body couldn't fit through that. Logan's eyes squinted in desperation as he continued to examine one of the pictures on the north wall. It was the image of a lion with a very angry look on its face. He knew he had seen this image before, but on a much smaller scale, like a tattoo or even a key chain. He gently hit his forehead with the palm of his hand as he attempted to jog his memory. The two officers approached, each carrying small evidence bags. "All right guys, let's head back to the station and see what we have."

*

Detective Logan was sitting at his desk with a pile of bloody pet collars and rusty knives, as the rest of the station was busy with activity. He carefully looked at each article, using rubber gloves and a small jeweler's lamp. The strange thing was that each collar still had the tag with the pet's names and the owner's address. He shrugged his shoulders in disbelief as he went through each name, one by one. There had been a long streak of pet abductions during the last eighteen months from Williams Bay subdivisions, and now the mystery had been solved as to what happened to them, but not who committed the crime.

The pet killings were extremely gruesome. Each animal was cut straight across the neck region, and there was virtually no blood in any of the carcasses. Some of the collars had been inadvertently cut, but not all the way through. He sat back in his chair for a moment to get a broad overview of the evidence sitting on his desk. "What in the world is going on here?"

An officer approached Logan's desk as he chewed on the end of his glasses. "Logan, a body just washed up on Williams Bay beach this afternoon."

Logan looked up. "An animal?"

"Human," the officer replied.

Logan got up from his desk and headed for the station door.

The entrance to the beach was littered with Walworth County and Williams Bay Township squad cars. A large group of bathers looked on in horror as Logan walked towards the covered body.

"Can we get these people out of here so we can do our jobs?" Logan snapped in frustration.

As several officers gestured for the crowd of onlookers to slowly move back from the scene, Logan carefully uncovered the black tarp covering the victim's face. He closed his eyes for moment as he tried to prepare himself for what he was about to see. As his hand slowly moved the plastic from the decaying flesh, the face of an elderly woman came into view. Logan's eyes were immediately drawn to the middle of the woman's forehead. The image of the angry lion that he saw in the room had been freshly imprinted on the woman's skin. He pulled the tarp down a little further to reveal the severity of the strangulation wounds around the woman's neck. He could hear the coroner's voice in the background, as his stomach grew increasingly weak. He carefully covered the body and waited for the coroner to approach the scene before he walked away.

*

Pastor Phil drove up the driveway of the Benedicts' home after receiving a call from Lynn that morning. Lynn opened the door to him. "Thanks, Phil, for coming over."

"No problem." He gave her a brief hug.

"John would be here, but he had a meeting with a client that he couldn't miss." She paused for a moment. "Would you like anything to drink?"

"No, I'm fine."

Lynn escorted him to the living room and they both sat down on opposite ends of a large coffee table. Lynn's body sank into a chair as she sighed heavily in exhaustion. "Phil, something just isn't right with Molly after her experience yesterday. I know what she went through was rough, but I can sense a change that doesn't fit her personality. I don't know if I'm just being a worried mother, or if I really am picking up on something. John and I are considering some counseling, but we want to talk with some trusted friends before we make that decision for her. You're one of those friends."

Phil sat up and put his Bible on the coffee table. "Lynn, I think counseling is a good idea, but the first thing we need to do is pray for God's wisdom in this situation. Have you and John been praying about this? I'm not talking about thanking him for keeping Molly safe from serious harm, I mean praying about spiritual protection. Rebuking any kind of spiritual influence that she may have come into contact with."

Lynn sat silent for a moment. "No, I can't say that we have specifically prayed for that."

Phil put his hands on the coffee table and smiled at Lynn. "Let's do that right now."

*

Detective Logan walked through the office doors of the juvenile crime department and examined a large shelf of records from past years. He remembered a drifter coming to Williams Bay during the late 1970s from the Chicago area. "Let's see here, 1978 and 1979," he murmured to himself. He pulled the thick folders from the shelf and opened the 1978 book. Most of the offenses were for shoplifting and drunk driving. He continued to page through the folder until something caught his eye. He took out a mug shot from May of 1978 and looked carefully at the hands of the man in the picture. Sure enough, there was an imprint of the same lion marking on the back of his hand.

"I knew I'd seen that tattoo before," he said to himself as he got up and checked the material out at the records counter. He sat back down at his own desk a started to sift through the file. The rap sheet on the individual was five pages long and most of the charges were misdemeanors. The personal information was sketchy at best, but there was a residence listed in Cicero, Illinois.

Logan dialed the number on the document and let it ring several times, but there was no answer. Then he reached for a phone book on his desk and started flipping through the yellow pages. "Here it is, tattoos." He wrote down the address and headed for the station door.

*

Molly Benedict got up from bed and walked towards the bathroom door as her mother started to get dinner ready. She turned down the lights as the steam began to fill the small room from the hot bath water. She dipped her right foot into the tub to check the temperature and slowly entered the water. She let her stitched hand hang over the edge as she sighed heavily in the comforting atmosphere.

Molly slowly drifted into a deep sleep as the water gradually became motionless in the porcelain tub. Her eyelids began to flutter a bit while her forehead dripped with sweat. A small drop fell from her chin and splashed into the steamy bath as her eyelids calmed down for a brief moment. She started to breathe heavily through her nose, as if her mouth were being smothered. Struggling to open her eyes, she violently kicked the end of the tub. Her lips exploded open for gasps of air while the stitched hand lunged for her throat.

Lynn could hear screaming in the distance and ran frantically to Molly's room. She wasn't there. She ran down the hallway shouting Molly's name. She noticed the bathroom door was closed. She grabbed the handle and turned it in desperation, but it was locked. She pounded on the door. "Molly! Molly! Open the door!"

She ran to her bedroom to get a hairpin, and nervously inserted it into the narrow hole on the knob and forced the door open. She saw Molly lying in the tub, fighting, with her eyes closed. Lynn stood frozen as she watched Molly struggle in the tub completely asleep. She took a firm hold of Molly's face to keep her mouth over the thick layer of bubbles. It was as if someone else was in the room pushing Molly's face under the water.

Lynn got in the tub and placed her hands under Molly's arms to lift her out of the water, and eventually managed to drag her onto the bathroom floor where she put several towels over her.

"Mom, why are you crying?" Molly asked, as she rubbed her neck.

John was just arriving back from work and could hear the commotion down the hall. He ran to the open bathroom door and comforted Lynn as she cried over Molly. "Lynn, what's wrong?" Then he saw Molly on the floor coughing and holding her neck.

Lynn's face looked terrified. "John, call Pastor Phil!"

CHAPTER FOUR

Logan approached the service counter of a tattoo shop in downtown Geneva and held up his badge. “My name is Detective Logan and I’m with the county sheriff’s department. Can I ask you about a drawing?”

A woman standing behind the counter agreed to answer whatever questions she could. Logan placed the picture of the lion on the counter and let the woman study the photo. “Have you ever seen this lion before?”

The woman surveyed the photo and turned her head in a curious manner. “I haven’t seen the lion before, but I’ve seen some of these other drawings. Where did you take this picture?”

“I really can’t answer that, seeing this is part of a pending investigation.”

The woman’s lips tightened as she looked at the

pictures one more time. She walked around the counter and removed a large three-ringed binder from a file cabinet. "Let me show you something," she said, motioning for Logan to come by the cabinet. She displayed several tattoo samples of demons and skulls that nearly matched the drawings on the wall. "These are a pretty close match, but some of these drawings were modified a bit. Most customers will pick something from a book and then modify it to their liking. It's rare for someone to find exactly what they want from our catalog."

Logan compared the photo to the pages, and noticed the category they were filed under. The title on the top of the page was labeled as *Occult*.

"Does your shop do much of this work?"

"Not really. We haven't had anyone ask for this style in a while. And I certainly don't recall anything recent," the woman replied, as she opened the file cabinet.

Logan placed his card on the counter. "Please give me a call if you come across anything."

The woman studied the card thoughtfully. "I sure will."

*

Pastor Phil's car entered the Benedicts' driveway and

John was there to greet him by the garage. “Thanks for coming again, Phil.”

Phil walked directly behind John as they entered the house. Lynn was stroking Molly’s hair on the couch as her head lay on a pillow in her lap. Phil walked straight over to Molly and Lynn and sat on the carpet. “Molly, it’s Pastor Phil. How are you doing?”

Molly looked up and smiled. “I guess okay. I just don’t know what’s happening to me.”

Phil put his Bible down and took out a sealed vial of oil from his shirt pocket. He dipped his finger in the oil and gently rubbed it on Molly’s forehead. He motioned for John to come by his side. “I want both of you to put your hands on Molly while I pray.”

All three of them placed their hands on Molly as Phil sat for a moment to collect his thoughts.

“Father, this family belongs to you and we pray that your Holy Spirit will fill this home. Satan has no business here and we order his demons to leave this place immediately. We rebuke any demonic spirit or influence from Molly’s life in the name of Jesus. Father, place your angels around this young lady’s life, and her family. The Benedict family is covered by the blood of Jesus Christ, and that means Satan has no authority here. We pray for your protection both spiritually and physically, and ask this in Jesus' name. Amen."

Phil paused for a moment and then opened his eyes. "John, can you show me where the incident happened in the bathroom? I want to pray in there as well."

John stood up and walked Phil to the bathroom. "Phil," he asked, "what do you think is going on here?"

Phil looked at the bathtub and leaned against the sink. "I believe Molly came in contact with some demonic forces in that house. I don't know exactly what she saw in the room, but from what you describe to me it sounds like satanic activity."

John had a shocked look on his face. "Are you saying that Molly is possessed?"

Phil quickly shook his head. "No, I'm not saying that she's possessed, but I do think there's a spiritual battle taking place in her life. I need you to tell me in detail what happened yesterday in that house."

*

Detective Logan arrived back at the station and noticed the autopsy report on the drowned woman on his desk. He opened the envelope and started rummaging through all the papers. The cause of death was listed as suffocation and blunt trauma. Dental records revealed the woman's name to be Lauren Delano of Highland Park, Illinois.

His thoughts were quickly interrupted by the station's public address system. "Detective Logan, call holding on line four. Detective Logan, line four."

Logan picked up the phone. "This is Detective Logan."

"Detective Logan, this is Tim at the Illinois Department of Motor Vehicles. I'm calling you back about your request for current information on a one Samuel Morelli of Cicero, Illinois. I didn't find much in the D.M.V.'s database, however the state records in Springfield shows that Mr. Morelli died in 1983."

"Do you show the cause of death?" Logan asked with frustration.

"He was suffocated."

Logan quickly sat up. "Suffocated?"

"That's what it says."

Logan started to write frantically on a note pad. "Can I get a copy of his state file?"

"Sure, you should have it in a few days," the voice on other end replied. "Where do you want it sent to?"

Logan put his other hand on the phone. "Hold on, I'm going to transfer you to our records department and they can tell you where to send it. And by the way, thanks for your help."

Click.

*

The next morning John and Lynn were eating breakfast in the kitchen, when the doorbell rang. John opened the door and Logan stood on the porch with his badge showing.

"Mr. Benedict, I'm Detective Logan with the county sheriff's department. Am I interrupting anything right now?"

"No. My wife and I were just having some breakfast."

Logan looked embarrassed. "I can come back later."

John motioned for Logan to come in. "No problem. Would you like some coffee?"

Logan smiled. "That would be great."

Lynn walked into the living room to see who it was. John could sense a little tension. "Honey, this is Detective Logan with the sheriff's department."

Lynn smiled and shook Logan's hand. "Pleased to meet you."

"I want to thank you both for letting me in your house," Logan said politely. "I was wondering if I could ask you some questions about the old Kholton estate on Black Point."

Lynn placed a mug of coffee on the table in front of Logan. "Thank you very much." Logan smiled at Lynn and then focused his attention on a note pad sitting on his lap. "From what I understand, you were the primary realtor for the Kholton estate when it was sold in May. Is that correct?"

John sat back in the chair and folded his legs. "That's correct."

"Can you give me a little background information on this property?" Logan asked, after taking a long sip of coffee.

"Well, it had been abandoned for at least ten years, and there was talk about the house being torn down for development. But the county planning board put a halt on any building, due to a pending request to give the house landmark status."

Logan looked puzzled. "What do you mean, landmark status?"

"Because the house is one of the oldest mansions on the lake, there was a small group of old-timers that wanted the state to offer the property protection from being demolished. There were several possibilities put on the table, including the State of Wisconsin taking it over and possibly making it into a museum. But no firm plans had ever been decided on for the property, and as a result the estate remained vacant for roughly a decade. The lake front acreage is some of the finest land on the whole lake, and that's where the real value lies. It's the land, not the house itself."

"Do you know who owned the property before Mr. Fossberg purchased it?" Logan asked, while writing down some notes.

"When the Fossbergs closed on the house, the only representative that showed up at the bank from the seller's side was a lawyer from Chicago. Apparently the house had been placed in a trust of some kind, and if it were to be sold the money made from the sale would be placed directly in the trust. The lawyer signed on behalf of the seller, and the transfer of ownership went without a hitch."

Logan stopped writing for a moment. "Isn't that kind of an unusual transaction? That seems a bit strange that the owner of a huge piece of property wouldn't show up for the closing."

"It's not unheard of, but it is unusual. I've only experienced a closing like that one other time, and in that case it was a widow that passed away. I've been in the real estate business for twenty-five years and have seen some strange things, but the Kholton estate has been in the back of my mind since I sold it."

Logan looked intrigued. "Why is that?"

John sat up and uncrossed his legs. "The property had been on the market for almost ten years and is in extreme disrepair. Even the bigwigs from Chicago wouldn't touch it. Real estate brokers from this area called it the "White Elephant."

Logan smiled. "A white elephant?"

John went on to explain. "When large lake estates go on the market, most of them are bought by several different investors and then the land is parceled out for the construction of homes. Because original estate houses are usually so old and would take a fortune to restore, the investors mutually decide to remove the old structures and have the land rezoned. You need to look at it from a business standpoint. Why sell the property with one restored house, when you could sell several parcels of land with brand new homes at a huge mark-up?"

Logan listened with great intensity. "That's interesting."

"The Kholton estate is comprised of the Victorian mansion plus three other structures, but the real prize is the five acres of lake front property." John paused for a moment. "I hesitate to say this because I don't want to break the trust of any client, but I was amazed that Mr. Fossberg paid cash for the property."

Logan flipped a page in his notebook and continued to record every word. "Can I ask what he paid?"

John shook his head. "I can't tell you what the final closing price was, unless Mr. Fossberg agrees, but the asking price was $5.5 million."

Logan whistled in disbelief. "That's some serious money."

"I'll be honest with you in saying that a sale like that doesn't come along very often. It has really helped Lynn and me get even closer to our retirement dreams."

Logan smiled for a moment. "If you don't mind me asking, what are your plans?"

"Well, Lynn and I have always wanted to do some missions work. We'll see what God has in store for us."

Logan looked over John's shoulder as Molly walked into the living room. Logan rose to his feet and extended his hand. "You must be Molly?"

Molly shook Logan's hand and sat down on the floor next to John. John kissed the top of her head. "Honey, this is Detective Logan with the county sheriff's department."

Molly smiled weakly. "Nice to meet you."

Logan opened an empty page in his notebook and looked at John. "Do you mind if I ask Molly some questions?"

John looked at Molly. "Are you up for some questions?"

Molly nodded slowly. "Sure."

"Molly, can you let me know if you saw anyone else around the house other than the Fossbergs that day?"

Molly stared at Logan's shoes as she jogged her memory. "The only person I saw that day was Mr. Fossberg. I know he said that both he and his wife were going to a store, but I didn't see her before they left. The house is so big that I just assumed she was somewhere on the property."

"Do you think the Fossbergs had anything to do with this?" John asked.

"No, the Fossbergs aren't suspects. I'm just trying to find out if there was anyone out of the ordinary in the house."

Molly leaned against John's leg and rubbed her knee. "The weird thing about those drawings on the wall was that I've seen some of them before."

"What do you mean?" Logan asked, as he stopped writing.

"There's a group of kids at my high school that are into that stuff. They dress in gothic clothes and wear black makeup and draw some of those images in their notebooks during class. Some of them even have tattoos, and others have them painted on their leather jackets."

Logan took some photos out of his suit jacket. "Can you look at these and tell me if you've seen any of these drawings at school?"

Molly took the pictures and examined them on the floor. "I've seen this drawing of the skull, but there are a lot of kids that have skulls on clothing and earrings. The gothic movement is pretty popular in my school."

Logan took back the pictures and smiled at Molly. "I really appreciate you taking time to talk with me."

John could see Lynn waving to him from the kitchen doorway. "Molly, I think mom has your breakfast ready for you." John looked at Logan. "Did you have any other questions for her?"

"No, she's been a big help." Logan paused for brief moment. "I think someone is at your door."

John pulled the curtain back from the bay window and looked outside. "Oh, that's our pastor." He quickly got up from the chair and opened the door. "Hey, Phil."

Phil walked in and nodded to Logan sitting in the living room. John closed the door and offered Phil a chair. "Phil, this is Detective Logan with the county sheriff's department."

Logan stood up and shook Phil's hand, before going to the door. "Thanks, Mr. Benedict, I'll be in touch."

CHAPTER FIVE

Detective Logan returned to the station and started to organize all the information. He reached for the phone just as his name was being paged. "This is Logan." He leaned both elbows on his desk as he listened to the voice on the other line. "You're kidding? I'll be right down." He grabbed his suit coat and walked down a long corridor to the interrogation wing.

Two police officers greeted him as he opened the door to a room with a double glass mirror. He looked into the room through the mirror and saw a teenage boy dressed in black clothes and makeup. Logan looked at the two officers. "What's the deal on this guy?"

"We arrested him for shoplifting."

Logan looked upset. "So what's that to me?"

One of the officers approached the glass and pointed at the earring dangling from the boy's left ear. It was an exact copy of the skull drawing in the house. "Look familiar?"

Logan put his face closer to the window as he put on his glasses. "Can I talk with him?"

The officer smiled. "Well, we left a message at his parents' residence. You may want to hold off until they arrive."

Logan was growing impatient. "I'm not waiting for mommy and daddy to arrive."

The officer didn't respond. Logan walked into the room and set his glasses down on a table between him and the boy. "My name is Detective Logan with the sheriff's department."

The boy remained silent as he stared at the floor.

"Do you mind if I ask you some questions? I'm not here to ask you about the shoplifting. I just want to know where you got those earrings."

The boy's eyes seared with anger as he looked at Logan for the first time. "I don't have to tell you anything."

Logan leaned over the table and carefully grabbed the boy's chin. "Listen, you little punk. If you don't start talking to me, shoplifting is going to be the least of your worries."

The door opened as Logan let go of his chin. Two men walked in and stood on each side of the boy. One man was dressed in a business suit, while the other was wearing a mechanic's uniform that was being stretched by a massive beer gut. Logan stood straight up and recognized the man in the suit immediately. "Well, if it isn't Charlie Siles," Logan said with a snicker. "Don't tell me you're representing this kid?"

Charlie looked at the boy. "Did you tell him anything?"

The boy sat silent.

"Logan, you know better."

Logan picked up his glasses and started to open the door. "You tell me when your client is ready to talk."

Logan walked back to his work area and noticed an elderly man sitting by his desk. "Can I help you?"

The man looked up at Logan. "No, but I think I can help *you*."

Logan took his jacket off and placed it on the back of his chair. "What do you mean?"

"I was reading about the woman who washed up on the beach the other day, and saw the name listed in the article. I knew this woman personally many years ago, and I may have some insight that could help in your investigation."

Logan sat up and opened his notebook. "How so?"

The elderly man extended his hand. "My name is J.R. Rosenberg."

Logan gently shook the man's shaky hand. "Please to meet you Mr. Rosenberg."

"You can call me J.R. As I was saying, I read about the incident in an Illinois paper, and noticed that there was a request by your department for any information regarding the investigation."

Logan was trying to be polite, but he really couldn't tell if this guy knew something or just wanted to shoot the breeze. "Do you have some information?"

J.R. remained silent for a moment as he crossed his legs. "I'm a retired newspaper reporter from Wescott, Illinois and I knew Ms. Delano very well."

Logan started to take notes. "And how did you know the deceased?"

J.R. smiled. "Do you have a few moments? This could take a while."

Logan tried to squeeze out a laugh. "I've all the time you need."

*

John and Phil decided to take a drive along the lake

and talk about Molly's condition. John inhaled the fresh breeze emanating from the shoreline as he looked out the car window. "I don't know, Phil, something just doesn't seem right with this whole situation. How can an old house have this kind of an affect on my daughter?"

The pastor sighed. "John, I can't tell you exactly what happened in that house, but your daughter needs both you and Lynn more than ever before. You can love Molly with all your might, but the greatest favor you can offer her right now is prayer."

"Phil, both Lynn and I pray for Molly everyday."

"John, I don't doubt that you do, but you may need to add a whole new dimension to your discussions with God. Don't get me wrong, it's important to pray for a child's future spouse and what course in life they decide to take, but as Christians we have a spiritual target on our backs. Satan is just waiting to attack us in any way that he can, and I believe he is doing everything he can to get at Molly."

John drove the car into a parking lot that overlooked the lake and turned off the ignition. "What are you trying to say, Phil? Are you telling me that Molly is bringing this on herself."

"John, listen carefully to what I'm saying. Molly is

a fine Christian girl. You and Lynn have done a wonderful job raising her in a Christian environment, and that kind of upbringing is not going to be overlooked in the spiritual realm. Satan doesn't need to worry about those who don't have Christ in their lives, because he already has them right where he wants them. He goes after the Christians because they pose the biggest threat to his limited authority. I can't say for sure that Molly wouldn't be experiencing these challenges if she hadn't entered that house, but I firmly believe she discovered a spiritual hornets' nest when she stumbled upon that room."

John shook his head. "I'll be honest with you, Phil. I think what's the most difficult for me to deal with is that I really never thought my family would go through something like this. I know that sounds very arrogant to say, but I feel like this whole thing is out of my control and I just don't know how to handle it. Molly has been the strong one through this ordeal, but Lynn and I can't even sleep at night."

Phil listened to John with compassion. "John, have you ever thought about what God may be trying to teach you through all of this? I'm not saying that I speak directly for God, but just consider that he may be trying to advance your spiritual life to an even higher level." Phil paused for a moment as he glanced at the lake. "Has that thought ever crossed your mind?"

John sat silent and took a deep breath. "It would be one thing if the attacks were on me, but not my daughter."

"John, you're missing the point, and you still didn't answer my original question. Satan isn't going to attack what doesn't mean that much to a Christian, he's going to focus on the most sensitive areas of a believer's life." Phil tapped John's knee. "Now, I want you to answer my question about going to a higher level."

Tears started to roll down John's cheeks. "I don't know, Phil. I suppose anything is possible. I just want this thing to be over. Here I am, an elder in a church, and I'm crying in front of my pastor."

Phil laughed. "John, it's no sin to cry, especially in front of your pastor. If I were in your shoes I'd be riled-up as well. I just want you to be honest with yourself, and most importantly with God. He already knows your weaknesses, concerns and thoughts even before you know what they are." Phil watched the tears drip from John's face. "God has a great habit of taking bad situations and turning them into life changing experiences that not only strengthen the believer, but also allow that individual to see a whole new dynamic in their spiritual life."

John tried to muster some words over the tears, but instead looked out the window.

"John, you and I've known each other for a long time, and I consider it an honor to have you on the church board, but like the rest of us you're not perfect."

"Phil, I already know that."

"Sure, I realize that you know that fact, but it's one thing to know it and another thing to really believe it and apply that truth to your life. I'm not telling you to down play the power Satan has in this world, but I've seen many Christians give him more authority and credit than he deserves. Do you remember what I said when we prayed in your house the other day? I said that Satan is a defeated foe in a Christian's life. Does that mean he's not going to try and cause trouble in our lives? Of course not, but you're playing right into his hands if you get discouraged."

John wiped the tears from this face. "So where does that leave me?"

"Claim the power you have as a child of God. Perhaps for the first time in your life you are at a place where you need to just give it entirely to God." Phil let his words soak into John's mind. "Let me ask you a figurative question?"

John made eye contact as Phil collected his thoughts.

"Okay, John, let's say that God was a wall and as a Christian you were to always lean on that wall night and day and not rely on anything else to balance your life. What would happen if the wall moved? Would you fall flat on your face, or would you have something else to keep you standing?"

John frowned. "I'm not sure I get it."

"Okay, I know that's a ridiculous analogy but I firmly believe God wants his children to lean only on him and not have any other items in their lives that may have the appearance of stability. Do you see where I'm going?"

John smiled for the first time since they got in the car. "Yea, I see what you're saying. I just feel so helpless?"

"John, if you were to rely on your own strength you would be helpless. But in Christ you have the full power of an all knowing and loving God. For years I've seen you tell people these truths during funerals and other challenges, but you may be realizing this for the first time in your own life. I wouldn't be telling you this if I didn't really care about you as a friend and a spiritual brother."

"I want to pray about this right now," John said under his tears.

Phil smiled and grabbed John's hand. "Let's go to war."

*

It was early evening and Detective Logan was at home eating dinner in front of the TV. The phone rang and he moaned in exhaustion as he reached for the remote. "Logan here."

He put down his fork as he listened to the voice on the other end. "I don't believe it," he said. "When did this happen? All right, I'll be right down."

He was behind the wheel of his cruiser, approaching the lakefront district of Williams Bay. He could see the blinding array of shooting lights from the squad cars parked in front of the municipal beach as he quickly arrived on the scene. He clipped on his badge and ran to the small army of onlookers staring at the body bag lying in the sand. Logan pulled the plastic sheet from the victim's face and sighed. "That's the kid we interrogated this afternoon for shoplifting."

An officer stood directly behind Logan to keep the

crowd away from the body.

"What's the cause of death?" Logan asked.

The officer looked at Logan. "Pull the plastic down about another six inches and you'll see."

Logan gently revealed a collapsed windpipe and a series of bloody rope marks around the victim's neck. Logan put on his glasses and took a closer look at the boy's wounds. His upper lip started to tremble as he grabbed the sleeve of the officer standing behind him. He pointed at the victim's neck, "That's the same lion imprint that we found on the Delano body."

The officer knelt down next to Logan. "That's why I called you down here." The officer took the plastic from Logan's fingers and recovered the body. "Detective, it looks like we have a serial killer on our hands."

CHAPTER SIX

Logan was up early the next morning, nursing a cup of black coffee while mulling over the murders. He stared at his backyard from the patio, watching the weeds grow from weeks of procrastination. He normally loved to work around the house, but the first murder had become an obsession of haunting proportions – and now there was another. He couldn't help but daydream about the faces of the two victims lying in front of him on the sand. He had seen many gruesome situations in his eighteen years on the force, but these murders touched a nerve.

The cordless phone sitting on the patio table started to ring as he sighed over the steamy coffee mug. "This is Logan." The blue veins in his forehead began to protrude from his wrinkled skin as he listened to the voice on the other line. "Tell the mayor

I'll be right down." He jumped to his feet and reached for the car keys in his coat pocket.

*

John Benedict was sitting in his car overlooking the lake from a picnic area while the sun shimmered on the dewy shoreline. Tears streamed down his face as he finished his morning devotions and pondered Pastor Phil's words from the day before. He knew changes needed to happen in his life, but he also needed to lead the way for changes in his family's life as well. For the first time he didn't feel prepared to face the obstacles sitting in his path.

In the business world his organizational skills led him to successes he had never dreamed of, but his family was becoming a whole other matter of concern. There were issues that had never come up until now, and weaknesses that were always there but were never really analyzed until this attack crossed his wake. John could taste the salt of his tears as the drops soaked his lips.

"Father, I know there are areas of my life that are being exposed for the first time. I was angry and frustrated that you didn't take them from me, but I'm starting to see the cracks they are exposing in my heart. For years I gave people advice and comforted their fears, thinking that I'd probably never taste the same type of pain in my life, but I'm plainly seeing how wrong I've been. I've come to the humble understanding that you have been so patient with me despite all my flaws. I'm also realizing that you really do accept me for who I am, but you love me too much to leave me as that same weak person. God, I can't do this on my own, and you know how hard it is for me to say those words, but it's true. Please go before me and make the paths smooth as I take a journey that will certainly bring me closer to the man you had always planned for me to be in your sovereign will. Gracious Father, you alone hold the keys to these locked doors, and I ask for the direction needed to walk through the right one. I love you, Father, in Jesus' name. Amen."

John opened his eyes and looked through the windshield of his car. The lake was as smooth as a mirror, and the sun's reflection looked like a magnificent fire on the water's edge. He knew there was serious spiritual work to be done, but he didn't have to do it all on his own. He knew that Jesus was just waiting for him to ask for help.

*

Detective Logan drove into the police station parking lot to be greeted by a barrage of portable TV cameras and news reporters. He exited the car and started to push away all the talking bodies in front of his path to the station door. He weaved around all the news vans littering the parking lot that had come from Chicago, Milwaukee and Madison. Logan's cheeks became red as he stared at the mayor's face viewing the spectacle from the main entrance of the police station. He walked straight up the intimidating stairs of the municipal building and turned around to view all of the commotion.

Williams Bay Mayor, Troy Becker, had a concerned look on his face as he opened the glass door to the lobby. "Logan, we need to talk about the murder investigation. As you can see, we have some outside interest regarding these matters."

Logan directed the mayor to follow him as they walked to an empty conference room. "Mayor, I don't know what to tell you at the present moment, but this is the last thing I need right now."

The mayor sat down at the head of the table and put his hands up in the air. "Logan, we need to work on this together."

Logan was puzzled. "Work on what together? The media circus, or the murders?"

"Both," the mayor replied.

"Mayor, if you think I've been dragging my feet on this case, then you can assign someone else. I'm getting too old for this kind of stuff."

"Logan, no one is kicking you off the case, but you and I need to start communicating about any current events relating to these murders."

"Does the chief know what's going on down here?"

The mayor nodded. "We made the call about five minutes ago. He was in the shower."

Shouting could be heard in the hallway as the mayor's assistant entered the conference room. "Sir, they are ready for both of you."

"Who's ready for us?" Logan asked, with a hostile tone.

The mayor looked straight at Logan. "We need to do a press conference right now, to give the people of this town a sense of security."

Logan sat silent and stared at the mayor's face. "You are unbelievable. You didn't call me down here to talk, you called me here to get in front of all those people so I could be put through a meat grinder."

The mayor's face sank as Logan looked out the window. "Detective Logan, I need you to do this press conference. Now what are you going to tell them?"

Logan opened the door. "The truth."

The mayor stood up and ran for the door. "Logan!"

Logan's was assaulted by camera flashes and microphones as he pushed his way to a podium with the city seal on it standing in the middle of the lobby. He stood amazed as he took in the scene for the first time. The room was blanketed with people, wires and large microphones hanging from long metal poles. "I can't believe this is happening," he murmured under his breath. "If my old man could see me now. . ."

"Detective Logan, what do we know about the two victims?" a reporter called from the gallery.

"The elderly woman had a summer home on the lake, and the young man is a resident of Williams Bay. I really can't share any more beyond those facts. Next question."

"Detective, do you see any motive behind the killings?"

"Not at this time."

One of the reporters in the front row stood to her feet and waved frantically in front of the other news people. Logan laughed for a moment and pointed in her direction.

"Can you share anything of substance?" the reporter asked.

Logan admired her honesty but didn't like the fact that he was in the hot seat. "Let me put it this way. This is a small town and we're not used to seeing this type of crime in our community. I'm as shocked by these senseless killings as everyone else, but the truth is I don't know who committed them, and I certainly don't know the motive. The police department has evidence that links the two murders together, but again it comes down to motive. Once we can figure out what the motive is, chances are the rest is going to come into the picture." Logan stood silent for a moment. "I know you want to get as much information as you can, but I refuse to jeopardize our investigation. You need to understand that we can't share every little detail with you."

"Do you have any suspects in custody?"

Logan put his hands on top of the podium. "No."

The room became quiet as the reporters continued to write frantically in their notepads. The same reporter waved her hand in the air.

"Do you feel this is going to affect the local tourism?"

Logan laughed as he looked back at the mayor. "I think that is a question for our distinguished mayor, Troy Becker." Logan waved Becker up as the camera flashes started to streak across the room.

Becker reluctantly walked to the podium as Logan stepped aside. The mayor's face was turning red as a rush of questions came from the gallery.

Logan walked to the back of the crowd and was on a mission to make his way to the lobby door. He headed down the massive concrete stairs in front of the station and noticed a young girl sitting on the last step. She looked up to see who was coming, and immediately rose to her feet. Her attire was identical to the boy he interrogated for shoplifting.

"Are you Detective Logan?"

"I am," Logan responded as he leaned against the handrail.

Tears started to roll down the girl's cheeks as she took off her leather jacket. Her arms were covered with tattoos of skulls and oddly shaped stars. "The guy you found on the beach last night was my boyfriend. I was supposed to meet him."

"So you where the one who dialed 911. Why did you leave the scene?"

"Are you kidding? The police would have been all over me. The group I hang around with is not exactly considered pillars of the community."

Logan took a handkerchief from his pocket and

gave it to the girl. "And what group is that?"

"We call ourselves the Outcasts," the girl replied, as she wiped her face.

"The Outcasts? What kind of name is that?"

"Just leave it alone," she said with scowl.

Logan wasn't sure if he was wasting his time or if she had something to share about the case. "Is there something I can help you with? I'm sorry, I didn't catch your name."

"I never told you what it was. My name is Sarah."

"Well, Sarah, what can I do for you?"

"I wanted to tell you that I think Brian's murder has something to do with the house on Black Point."

"What do you mean?" Logan asked with a confused look.

"The lion marking on Brian's neck was put on him when he was killed," Sarah said, as the tears continued to pour down her cheeks.

"Are you sure? I don't mean to be disrespectful, but Brian had numerous markings on his body. Isn't there anyway you could have missed one?"

Sarah looked angry. "Listen, I was his girlfriend. Get it? Don't you think I'd know what markings were on his neck?"

"I get your point," Logan said with a heavy sigh.

"The only time I had ever seen that marking was in the Black Point house. I read in the paper that the girl who tore down the wall and found the secret room discovered the dead animals. That was the room where I first saw the lion."

"Was your group responsible for that?" Logan asked with raised eyebrows.

Sarah's face was soaked with tears as she sat back down on the steps. "Brian and I where there when they killed those animals, but we wanted to leave the group after that night. I'll admit that I've done some strange things, but I'd never kill animals for the fun of it."

"You expect me to believe that you had nothing to do with what happened to those animals?"

"Look, old man, I came to you. Do you want to hear what I have to say?"

Logan looked at his car in the parking lot. "Do you want something to eat? Of course I'd like to hear what you have to say, but just not on the front steps of the station. That mob will be coming out any minute and I just can't answer another pointless question."

Sarah seemed hesitant as she looked around in a paranoid manner. "Okay, but can we go somewhere outside of Williams Bay? I don't want any of my friends seeing me talk with a cop."

Logan took out his car keys. "Fair enough."

*

John Benedict walked into the kitchen as Lynn finished a bowl of cereal. "John, why aren't you at the office?" She could tell he had been crying. "John, are you okay?"

"Lynn, I need to talk with you and Molly."

Lynn walked to the hallway and knocked on Molly's bedroom door. "Honey, are you up yet?"

Molly walked out of the room in her pajamas, startled by her father's appearance. "Dad, are you all right?"

John motioned for both Molly and Lynn to sit with him on the living room couch. "I've come to the realization that I've been failing as a husband and a father."

Molly and Lynn tried to interrupt, but John wouldn't let them.

"Let me finish." He wiped some tears from his eyes as he leaned forward. "I've tried to keep this house under my control, because I believed that was what a man should do. And in doing that I've opened our family to outside influences that are trying to tear it apart." He looked at Molly as she rubbed her neck.

"I've been convicted to make some serious changes as a husband and father. I have also been reminded that this is God's family, and that my relationship with each of you is a gift that could be taken away at any time. If I try to keep this family under my control, I could lose it. But if I give this family entirely to God, it will be taken care of in a way that I could never accomplish."

He paused and put his arms around both Molly and Lynn.

"I can't help but think that I'm partly responsible for what happened to you, Molly. I'm realizing that decisions made, or not made, in life have a much stronger impact than I first thought."

Lynn and Molly watched John cry as his strong arms trembled on their shoulders. Molly wanted to say something, but she could see her mother looking at her with an expression on her face that was all too clear.

"Let him cry, Molly. Let him cry," Lynn said softly as she rubbed her husband's hand. "John, it's an honor to be your wife."

Molly's eyes were overwhelmed with tears. "Dad, it's not your fault. I should have never gone in that room. Please don't blame yourself."

John could sense a healing with his family, but he could also recognize a peace that he had never experienced before. The pain was still there, but the feeling of being alone was completely gone. He knew that growth would have its challenges, but the prospect of that growth didn't terrify him anymore. Being able to show his wife and his daughter that he didn't always have the answers was a relief that had no explanation. He had finally handed over the keys to his family, and those keys were now in God's hands.

CHAPTER SEVEN

Detective Logan walked back into the station after having breakfast with Sarah, the girl who had stopped him on the front steps of the station. Her conversation opened his eyes concerning the juvenile problem in the community, but he couldn't help but think she was trying to work him for information instead of offering help in his investigation. Logan's thoughts were heavy and numerous as he processed the details in his mind. What would a grungy high school kid and a harmless old woman have in common?

He walked up to his cubicle and noticed a stack of messages from the desk sergeant. He sighed as he slowly eased into the chair and started to rummage through the stack of notes and phone numbers. J.R. Rosenberg's name caught his eye on one of the messages, but the phone number for the retired reporter was local, not from Illinois.

"Mr. Rosenberg is back in the area," he whispered to himself, remembering his recent meeting with the man who claimed to know the murder victim, Lauren Delano, very well. He called the number and was answered by a hotel front desk. "Yes, may I have Mr. Rosenberg's room? Thank you."

Logan waited for Rosenberg to answer. "Mr. Rosenberg, I received your message. What can I do for you?" Logan glanced at his watch with a perturbed expression. "Okay, Mr. Rosenberg, I'll meet you down at the library in about an hour. See you then."

Click.

Logan rubbed his eyes with the bottom of his hand. "Things just don't add up."

*

Detective Logan could see Rosenberg waiting in the library parking lot as he exited his car. He smiled at the old man's soft wrinkly face. "How are you doing?"

Rosenberg had a serious look in his eyes as he took a sealed package and a battered briefcase from his car. "Detective Logan, I received this package in the mail today from Lauren Delano. I've not opened it."

Logan looked at it and noticed that it had been

postmarked two days before Lauren's murder.

He and Rosenberg entered the library and walked to a private reading room towards the back of the periodical section. Rosenberg was clearly shaken as he held the large envelope in his weathered hands. Logan pulled out a chair and sat directly across from the retired reporter.

"Detective, something tells me there are answers in this package that pertain to her murder."

Logan was curious about the contents. "Do you want me to open it?"

Rosenberg nodded grimly.

Logan gently took the envelope from Rosenberg's hands and slowly tore the paper open. He dumped the contents on the table and out fell a brass key and a gold ring. Logan picked up the ring and noticed that it bore the strange lion imprint. "Well, I'll be. . ." Logan began, as he analyzed the piece of jewelry.

"You will know what to do with these," Rosenberg said, as he read a brief note that came from the envelope.

"Do you know what these are for?" Logan asked, as he watched Rosenberg re-read the note.

"No," Rosenberg responded in confusion. "But I brought some old articles that pertain to Lauren and what her relationship was with the Kholton family."

"What do you mean? What connection did she have with the Kholton family?"

Rosenberg opened his old briefcase and laid out a tattered scrapbook. "Detective, I need you to bear with me as I gather my thoughts. It was many years ago when all this happened, but I think Lauren's death has everything to do with her past."

Logan was intrigued as he helped Rosenberg organize the vintage news clippings. "Why didn't you tell me some of this in our previous meeting?"

"To tell you the truth, Detective, my mind is a little rusty. Things started coming back to me as I tried to remember some of the highlights of my investigation with Kholton. My newspaper articles were partly to blame for a corporate downfall that was the talk of the town during my day." Rosenberg took out an article and laid it in front of Logan. "Lauren was the daughter of a very powerful businessman who just happened to be Jack Kholton's partner."

"Are you talking about the Kholton Agriculture scandal of the 1940s?"

"Are you familiar what that incident?" Rosenberg asked, a surprised look on his face.

"I can't say I know every detail, but my parents

would mention it from time to time when reminiscing about days gone by."

Rosenberg leaned back in his chair as he prepared to share something serious with Logan. "That scandal was partly responsible for putting our country into the Great Depression. Lauren's parents were both killed by Kholton's henchmen when she was just a teenager. Even though Lauren was just a kid at the time, she was made the sole beneficiary of her father's empire. The only problem was that Kholton had taken everything before he had Lauren's father killed. She had been on the run for several years until I stumbled upon her during a routine investigation." He paused and smiled at Logan. "I was a young starving reporter in Wescott, Illinois back then, and that investigation basically shaped my career. Anyway, Kholton's men had been after Lauren for a long time, because she was the only one who could identify the killers. But they were also convinced that she possessed secret documents that her father had hidden from Kholton that pertained to a slush fund. Those documents were never found."

Logan sat back and listened to every word as if it were a novel being read to him for the first time. "What ever happened to Kholton?"

"He was assassinated by one of his own."

"By one of his own?" Logan asked with a shocked tone.

"Kholton was a cruel man and was thought to have had ties to Nazi Germany even before the war broke out, but that was never really confirmed. That estate on Black Point was a popular hangout for Jack Kholton, and I can't help but think that Lauren was up here now to visit that house."

"Do you think Kholton's men weren't necessarily after papers all that time, but rather this?" Logan asked, as he looked over the odd-looking key.

"I really don't know. But I'll say it's strange that Lauren would send me these things after all these years. We kept in touch, but it certainly wasn't a close relationship. In some ways I was the only family that she had, because of the investigation and all, but it's odd that she'd send me this stuff."

Logan continued to study the key. "The police department uses a locksmith here in town when we require that kind of service. Would you mind if I show him this key and see if he has any idea what it might open?"

"Take the key and the ring. I don't know what Lauren was up to when she mailed me these items, but she must have had a good reason. I just wish I knew what the reason was," Rosenberg said with frustration.

"Hopefully we'll find out soon enough," Logan said as he put the two items back into the envelope.

*

Molly Benedict was stretching on the front lawn to prepare for a jog late that afternoon. Her thoughts were still on her dad and how he had reacted to the whole incident with the Black Point estate. She had never seen him cry in that manner before and it made her feel a bit uneasy. As she began to run down one of the sidewalks towards town she started to feel free and alive as the gentle breeze hit her sweaty forehead. The smell of fresh cut grass saturated the air as kids rode their bikes in the streets. She turned down a side street to get a little more privacy just as a van appeared directly behind her.

Whoever was driving the van was keeping the same distance, even though there was plenty of room to pass. Molly stopped running and stared at the white van as it gradually approached her area of the street. She started to jog back towards home, but the van came up alongside and drove right in front of her path. The side-door opened and two men with ski masks grasped her arms, and dragged her body to the open door.

"*No!*" Molly screamed, hoping someone would hear her plea for help. She started to bite the fingers covering her lips, prompting one of the men to yell in agony as she penetrated the leather glove on his hand. The other man grabbed her feet and they both carried her to the side-door on the van. Molly's head hit the floor and she noticed the shadow of another person leaning against the van wall, bound and gagged.

One man blindfolded Molly and the other kidnapper bound her hands and legs as the weight of the van shifted violently from the driver's panicked steering maneuvers. Molly tried to kick whatever her feet would touch, but the men were just too strong for her to gain any kind of freedom from their clutches.

The two men leaned Molly next to the other kidnapped passenger as the van's speed increased with every tense second. She felt the body next to her tremble as the van came to a stop. She could make out the familiar sounds of the Williams Bay beach as the van idled at a traffic light. She tried to scream in desperation, but the tight rag covering her mouth absorbed any words that she could muster. Then the van started to accelerate and the comforting sounds of the town grew weaker as the sobs of her bound neighbor became more intense with every endless mile.

*

Logan walked into the town's locksmith shop hoping he could find out more on the mysterious key. A golden retriever greeted him as he rang the bell at the service counter.

An old man entered the room from behind a curtain and saw Logan petting the dog. "Can I help you?"

Logan took the key out of his pocket and placed it on the counter. "I was wondering if you could tell me something about this."

The old man's arthritic hands slowly picked up the brass key as he turned on a work light. "It certainly isn't domestic. I'd say it's from Europe, perhaps made before the war."

"What makes you say that?" Logan asked.

The old man motioned for Logan to come closer as he shined the light directly on the key. "See those markings near the bottom grooves?" The locksmith's shaky hands pointed directly at a series of numbers and letters that could barely be seen with the naked eye. "I need to take this into the back and look it over with a magnifying lamp," the old timer said, as he disappeared behind the curtain.

Logan marveled at the store's inventory of antique doorknobs, dead-bolts and keys. The wood-planked floor was covered in paw prints as the dog made its regular rounds in and out of the small aisles. Logan could hear the old man shuffling his steps as he reappeared from behind the curtain. He handed Logan the key and immediately turned around to face a large collection of books sitting on a dusty shelf. The locksmith placed a large catalog on the counter and started flipping through a series of faded pages.

"Here it is," he said, as he turned the book around so Logan could read the description. "It's a German key typically used in small house safes, but this one is not your normal, run-of-the-mill safe key." He paused and pointed to the end of the key. "The tiny grooves on the bottom tell me that whatever safe this key belongs to also uses a combination lock as well." He closed the book and looked at Logan. "Those Germans were excellent engineers, and I know that for a fact, because I fought them in the war."

Logan smiled as he looked at the locksmith's wrinkled face. "I can't thank you enough for you services. What do I owe you?"

"Forget about it. I didn't do anything except look up a few numbers."

"Thanks again," Logan said with a grin as he walked out of the shop.

*

Detective Logan promised Rosenberg a visit at the hotel once he found out the nature of the key. He drove into the parking lot of the Green Acres Resort and noticed a swarm of squad cars surrounding a corner room facing the pool. The detective parked his car near a running police cruiser and ran to the hotel room that was the focus of attention. He pushed his way through the crowd of hotel guests as one of the police officers greeted him with a somber look.

"What happened? Why didn't anyone notify me on the radio?" Logan yelled.

"We tried, but we didn't get a response."

Logan remembered turning off his radio when he visited the locksmith. "So what happened?"

The officers flipped through pages of notes. "According to two witnesses, a late model white Ford van approached a Mr. J.R. Rosenberg when he was trying to enter his hotel room around 3:45 P.M. The witnesses stated that two men wearing black clothes and ski masks walked up to the victim, grabbed both his arms and dragged him into the van. The van exited the parking lot heading east on Highway 67 towards the town of Geneva."

"Did anyone get a look at the plates?" Logan asked, as he made his way over to Rosenberg's room.

"There were no plates on the vehicle," the officer answered. "Did you know the victim, Detective?"

Logan put on a pair of rubber gloves and started to search the room for any evidence. "As a matter of fact I did. He's been helping me with the murder cases. Did he even get in the room before they grabbed him?"

"Not that we're aware of," the officer replied cautiously as he glanced at Logan's angry face.

Logan was visibly angry. "Can you guys get out there and start asking questions? There are twenty potential witnesses standing out in the parking lot, and one of them had to have seen something."

Logan stood motionless in front of the mirror and stared at the veins protruding from his forehead. He sat on the bed to contain his emotions and noticed Rosenberg's briefcase leaning against the dresser near the bathroom door. "He must have been in here before they took him," he whispered to himself. He picked up the badly damaged briefcase and looked inside only to find that it had been cleaned out. “I can’t believe this is happening!” he screamed as he kicked a trash can across the room.

CHAPTER EIGHT

John Benedict walked the sidewalk in front of his house and looked down both ends of the street. He could see a few kids riding their bikes and one of his neighbors washing a car, but no sign of Molly. He glanced at his watch and realized that she had been gone for nearly two hours. He ran back into the house and grabbed his car keys hanging in the entryway. "Lynn, I'll be back in a few minutes," he yelled, as he closed the front door.

"Okay, honey," Lynn replied as she put some laundry in the dryer.

John's stomach was in knots as he started the car. He didn't want to panic Lynn without cause, but it wasn't like Molly to be gone for more than an hour when she went for a jog.

He pulled the car up his neighbor's driveway and

rolled down the window. "Bob, have you seen Molly jogging around here?"

The neighbor put down a garden hose and leaned against John Benedict's Lincoln. "I saw her earlier this afternoon, running towards town."

"Thanks. I'll see you later," John said, as he drove away from the curb. He noticed that his knuckles were turning white as his fingers tightly gripped the leather wrapped steering wheel. He knew Molly's normal jogging route like the back of his hand and he had nearly finished the entire length of the four-mile course. He stopped the car in the middle of an intersection and turned down one of the wooded side streets.

He slammed on the brakes as he abruptly shifted the car into reverse. He drove back about one-fifth of a mile and quickly hit the brakes again as the car's front tires kicked out a heavy cloud of gravel dust. He ran to the rear bumper of the car and picked up a blue jogging shoe that was lying on the side of the road. He looked inside the shoe and noticed where Molly had written her initials with permanent marker on the side of the heel.

"*Molly! Molly!*" he screamed, as he frantically looked in the abandoned field next to the street. He walked back to the car and tripped in a deep tire rut on the soft gravel shoulder. Tears started to roll down his face as he tightly held Molly's shoe. "God, please help me!"

*

Logan walked back to his car and started to write down a few notes. He flipped on the police scanner hanging on the car's dashboard and turned the volume down as a flood of voices came across the speaker. The detective put down his pen and turned the scanner's volume back up as the Benedict name caught his attention. He looked up from his notepad and noticed two squad cars pulling out of the hotel parking lot to answer the new scanner call. He revved his engine and followed directly behind the second cruiser as all three cars made their way to the opposite side of town.

Logan placed the small cherry light on top of the roof as a set of sirens screamed in unison from the two lead cars. All three cruisers quickly approached the driveway of the Benedict home as John and Lynn sat on the steps of the porch with tear-stained faces. John stood up and greeted Logan and the two officers as they made the trek across the small front lawn.

Logan was the first to shake John's hand. "Mr.

Benedict, I need you to calm down and tell me exactly what happened."

"How can you expect me to calm down when my little girl could be dead right now!" John retorted in anger.

Logan put his hand on John's shoulder as he tried to offer some comfort. "Please, tell me whatever you can."

John was trying to hold back his tears. "Molly went out for jog about two hours ago and didn't come back. She's never gone that long and she always takes the same route. The whole run should take about forty-five minutes."

"What makes you think she was kidnapped?" Logan asked, as he wrote down every detail.

John took the shoe from Lynn's hands and gave it to Logan. "I found this on a wooded side street near a set of tire ruts and skid marks." He opened the shoe and showed Logan the initials Molly wrote on the heel.

Logan looked at the two officers. "Guys, I want you to stay with Mrs. Benedict while John and I go back to the scene."

Logan's car tore down the street as neighbors stood motionless on the sidewalk watching all the activity in front of the Benedict home. John pointed at the intersection where Logan needed to make a right turn and both men sat straight up in their seats to find the precise location of the tire marks. "There they are," John yelled, and Logan pulled the car onto the gravel shoulder.

Logan picked up his police radio and gave the dispatcher his location. "This is Logan. I need a K-9 unit on Park Ridge Circle in the Cedar Point subdivision. Do you copy? Over."

Heavy static came across the radio speaker followed by a series of clicks. "I copy you, Detective. A K-9 unit is being dispatched to your location. Copy? Over."

Logan raised the radio up to his mouth. "I copy you. Over."

Logan and John started to search through the long grass of an abandoned lot as the echo of sirens bellowed in the distance. John's hands were trembling as he ran frantically to one corner of the huge field while Logan ran back to his cruiser and flagged down the approaching squad cars.

A cruiser approached the scene in a thick cloud of dust as it came to an abrupt halt on the dry gravel. Two officers ran directly to the back of the vehicle to retrieve the dog as Logan grabbed Molly's shoe from the front seat of his car. He opened the shoe wide open and shoved it in a German Shepherd's face. "Go get her, boy!" Logan yelled, as the dog disappeared into the long dense grass.

John walked back from the field and approached Logan leaning on his car. Logan was trying to think of something to say, but no words came to his mind as he watched the stress take its toll on John. "Mr. Benedict, I need to tell you something, but I need you to keep this under your hat."

John shook his head in agreement.

"Mr. Benedict, before I arrived at your house a few minutes ago I had just come from the Green Acres Resort regarding a kidnapping incident. The missing victim was an elderly man from Illinois who was helping me with the murder investigation."

"What are you saying? Whoever has my daughter is going kill her?" John asked with terror.

"Mr. Benedict, I'm not saying anything like that. I wouldn't normally share this information with a civilian, but considering the coincidence of these two abductions I thought it was appropriate to tell you."

John kicked angrily some gravel onto the road. "Why would they take Molly? It just doesn't make sense."

Logan bit his lip as he watched John agonize over the situation. "Mr. Benedict, please get in the car. I'm going to drive you home and explain to you some of things that I think your daughter may have inadvertently come in contact with."

Logan drove back to the Benedict home and parked directly behind the two police cruisers. Lynn was in the living room, with a clump of tissue in her left hand as she talked with the two officers. She immediately rose to her feet when she saw John and Logan approach the house from the view of the bay window that overlooked the front lawn. "What happened?"

John grabbed Lynn's hand and escorted her to the couch. Tears poured from her eyes as she expected the worst. "Please tell me what happened."

Logan sat down directly across from John and Lynn and cleared his throat as he prepared himself to share the information. "Mr. and Mrs. Benedict, as you have probably heard, there have been two murders within the Williams Bay city limits during the past few days. These murders are linked together. However, at this time we don't know the motive and unfortunately we don't have any suspects. There was another kidnapping that happened this afternoon at a resort outside of town. The victim was an older man who knew the woman who was killed last week." Logan paused to catch his breath. "I was talking with him this afternoon, and within a few hours the call came in that he had been abducted."

"Detective, what do these people want with my daughter?" Lynn asked, under the tears.

"Mrs. Benedict, I don't know. But I'm going to do everything I can to find out. I want to ask you if you've noticed anything unusual during the last few days. I know I spoke with you last week about the Black Point incident, but has there been anything beyond that?"

John raised his hands to interrupt Logan's sentence. "You don't think this has anything to do with that house?"

Logan was hesitant to answer. "It's possible."

John face was turning a deeper shade of red with every word that came out of Logan's mouth. "What do you mean? Why would that house have anything to do with Molly?"

"I have reason to believe that the recent crime spree is somehow linked to the Kholton property."

"How so?" John asked, as he put his arm around Lynn.

"Mr. Benedict, how much do you really know about the people who bought that house?"

"Cameron and Morgan Fossberg? What do they have to do with this?"

Logan was under the gun to answer, but wanted to make sure he didn't incriminate anyone without justifiable cause. "They probably have nothing to do with any of it, but the house does. I know it sounds crazy, but you have to believe what I'm telling you."

An officer walked into the front door and handed Logan an envelope.

"What's that?" Lynn asked, as she watched Logan read the documents.

Logan had a confident expression. "It's a search warrant. I'm going to look through the entire Black Point estate."

John stood up from the couch and stared at Logan. "I'm going with you."

Logan didn't answer right away. "I'll let you go, Mr. Benedict, but you need to stay in a car with an officer. I can't risk you getting involved if something happens in that house."

Lynn looked up at John as she continued to hold his hand. "Honey, I need you here."

"Lynn, I want you to call Pastor Phil and tell him

to come over here with some elders."

Lynn hesitantly agreed and walked to the phone.

John opened the front porch door as he watched Detective Logan walk out to the car. He noticed tears roll down Lynn's face as she hung up the phone. "I love you," John said with a tender voice.

Lynn started to cry uncontrollably as John put his big arms around her petite body. "It's in God's hands," he whispered as he stroked his wife's thick auburn hair. "It's in God's hands."

*

Molly Benedict tried to control her tears, as a dark towel was unwrapped from her head. She readjusted her eyes to the new surroundings as she looked to her right and saw an old man lying unconscious with bloody lips. A burst of light flashed across the room as footsteps grew louder with every agonizing second.

"Hello, Molly. Welcome back," a voice said behind the light.

It took her a moment to recognize the voice. "Mr. Fossberg?" She didn't want to believe it was Cameron, but the voice was unmistakably his. The light was so blinding that she closed her eyes and looked towards the ground. The jagged wall dug into her shoulder blades, and her jogging suit was quickly absorbing whatever liquid was on the damp floor. The roar of an intense flame could be heard in the distance, accompanied by faint voices echoing off the walls.

"Molly, I need you to listen to me very carefully."

Molly started to cry as she listened to Cameron whisper the orders.

"Why are you doing this?" she asked with a trembling voice.

"Molly, please listen to me. I don't want to hurt you, but it's very important that you listen carefully." Cameron paused for a moment. "What did you see when you went into the room?"

Molly tried to answer through her tears, but her voice didn't have the strength to overcome the terror.

"Molly, I need you to focus. Let's try it again. Did you see a key when you entered the hidden room?"

"What are you talking about?"

Cameron sounded desperate. "Molly, *where is that key?*"

*

Detective Logan's car approached the entryway of the Kholton Estate and came to an abrupt halt. Three police cruisers idled behind his vehicle as he walked to an intimidating set of rusty gates that had recently been chained together. Logan stuck his head through the gate railings and searched the impressive lake front property hoping to see another way onto the estate.

John exited the car and approached Logan. "I know another way."

Logan slowly took his head out of the gate. "Where?"

"There's an access path on the west part of the property," John said, as he pointed down the road.

Logan bit his lip. "Show me."

*

Cameron Fossberg walked up to Rosenberg's body and kicked him in the ribs. "Wake up, old man! Wake up!"

Rosenberg started to cough as the intermittent kicks brought him to his senses. Cameron grabbed his shoulders and propped his body against the wall. "Old man, I have a surprise guest for you."

Rosenberg slowly opened his eyes and noticed Molly staring at him. "Oh, my dear child, I can't believe they brought you here." Rosenberg looked straight ahead as he spit out a mouthful of blood. A faint shadow approached both Rosenberg and Molly as the roar of a blowtorch kept resonating in the distance.

A thin, short man with silver hair and facial scars walked alongside of Cameron. “Well, Mr. Rosenberg, I find it terribly ironic that we meet again under such unusual circumstances,” the elderly man said, with a heavy German accent.

Rosenberg had a stunned look on his face. “Klaus Fossberg? Is that really you?”

“The one and only. I see my son introduced himself,” Klaus said with a snicker, as he wiped some blood from Rosenberg’s upper lip. “Why don’t you do everyone a favor and tell us where the key is.”

It took Rosenberg a few seconds to take in the fact that Klaus Fossberg was standing in front of him. Klaus had been Kholton’s right hand man and one of the most well respected hired guns for the Chicago mob families during the 1940s. Rosenberg sat silent as he recalled the past image of Klaus’s lifeless body lying in a Chicago alley after a violent gunfight on the city’s south side. It was one of Rosenberg’s first reporting assignments as a young police beat reporter. So how could the man be here now?

Rosenberg awoke from his thoughts and looked at Molly. “Let this girl go. She has nothing to do with this.”

Klaus looked at Cameron Fossberg with disgust.

"Why did you bring the girl? She's just a child."

Cameron stood silent as he stared at the ground.

"If you let her go, I'll tell you where the key is," Rosenberg said in desperation.

Klaus and Cameron laughed at Rosenberg's proposition. "Tell us first where the key is, and *then* we'll let her go," Cameron said as he looked at Molly.

Rosenberg was getting angry. "You won't. You'll kill us both if I tell you where it is."

Rosenberg was being manhandled like a piece of meat in a butcher shop as Cameron grabbed him by the shirt collar and dragged him toward the stairway leading toward the basement. His frail body slid from one stair to the next while his old leather shoes half dragged and half walked as he attempted to keep up with the frantic pace of his abductor.

Rosenberg squinted as he watched two individuals working over a large safe with blowtorches.

One of the men holding a torch doused the intense flame and removed the elaborate welding helmet from his matted hair. He looked at Klaus and Cameron with a frustrated glare. "I can't even make a dent in this thing."

Rosenberg smiled as he watched Cameron's face. "You'll never get the safe open without a key," he said with a grin.

Klaus walked up to Rosenberg and knelt down next to him. "Do you even know what's in there?" Klaus asked, as his steel blue eyes focused on the safe.

"I have no idea," Rosenberg replied.

Klaus was in no mood for chitchat. "Let me save you the time." He dragged Rosenberg over to an empty wine rack so he could face the safe. "This safe contains monetary printing plates that were minted in Germany during the war."

Rosenberg was puzzled. "German Marks?"

Klaus had a devious look on his face as he peered down at Rosenberg. "No. U.S. dollars." Klaus laughed as he watched Rosenberg's reaction. "You see, Mr. Rosenberg, the Nazis had a plan during the war to print billions of American dollars to devalue the U.S. currency." Klaus stopped for a moment and leaned against the safe. "We were fighting the war on many fronts, and with many different weapons."

"But the country was already in a depression," Rosenberg said, as he groaned in pain.

Klaus walked away from the safe. "I know, and the Nazis wanted to keep it that way."

Rosenberg stared at Klaus. "And you were the officer in charge of the conspiracy? Weren't you?"

"I was," Klaus said with pride.

"What else is in there?" Rosenberg asked.

"Approximately ten million dollars that would pass even the most stringent U.S. Treasury's standards."

Rosenberg started to piece together Lauren's involvement. "Why did you kill Lauren Delano?"

Klaus sat next to Rosenberg while leaning against the safe. "Lauren? That was an unfortunate incident that didn't have to happen."

Rosenberg felt himself beginning to shake with rage. "You didn't answer my question."

"Lauren's father was getting wind of Jack Kholton's ties with the Nazi revolution. I have to hand it to old man Delano. He remained faithful to his patriotic convictions, but they also put him in the grave. Everyone thought Lauren was being hounded all those years because she could identify the henchmen that killed her parents, but what they were after was the key to this safe. She had possessed that key all those years, but didn't have a clue as to its value." Klaus paused for a moment as he woke up from his day dreaming. "Kholton was Germany's point-man for this operation, but Delano was about to blow the whistle. No one ever knew the safe was taken here, except Kholton and myself. I'm just taking what's rightfully mine."

Rosenberg was trying to take it all in. "Klaus, you and I first met nearly fifty years ago on totally opposite sides of life, but we come from the same stock. I was a young reporter and you were Kholton's advisor, but our generation did things a little different. If you wanted the key, why didn't you just take it from Lauren?" Rosenberg tried to contain his emotions. "So much killing."

Klaus sat and listened to Rosenberg as he took a stroll down memory lane. "The war brought out the best and worst in our generation. America was the only bastion of hope that I had for my family back then, and I wasn't about to go down with Hitler's ship. Not many people knew that Nazi soldiers weren't only going after Jews, but after everyone who failed Hitler. I know this may sound hard to believe, but I never supported the Nazi movement. I was planning on coming to America, but I was dragged into the war and had two options set before me: go to America and see my family killed, or stay in Germany and take my chances."

Rosenberg tried to sit up. "You stole Hitler's money, didn't you?"

Klaus smiled. “Not a bad deduction, Mr. Rosenberg.”

“Everyone thought you were killed in that gun fight,” Rosenberg said with a curious tone. “I saw you lying in the street with my own eyes.”

“That was the point. That gunfight was staged to take the attention off Kholton’s activities. The police were paid off and the press was called to cover it.” Klaus looked at Rosenberg with a grin. “Some reporters took the story for what appeared to happen, and others had to dig a little further.”

Rosenberg was stunned. “Are you saying that I was hand-selected to cover the story because Kholton thought I’d just let the facts stand?”

“Kholton needed a diversion to get his political plans in motion but he underestimated one reporter from Wescott, Illinois.”

“But to wait all this time?” Rosenberg asked, as he tried to stretch his leg.

Klaus leaned closer to Rosenberg. “One thing you learn in the military is patience. I was on the losing side of one war over forty years ago, but I guarantee you I won't be this time.”

CHAPTER NINE

Three officers walked up behind Detective Logan's cruiser and waited for his instructions. He exited the front seat and looked at the uniformed officers as they checked their weapons. "One of you needs to stay here with Mr. Benedict while I search the property."

Logan and two officers started to walk down the path as the sun quickly set in the western sky. The access road was more or less a dirt trail wide enough for a car, but was covered by dense trees and completely hidden from the view of the house. The two officers were dressed in black with matching bulletproof vests, and Logan was wearing a dark trench coat and a fedora hat.

"I want one of you to be posted on the lake side of the house and the other on the back side," he whispered. The two officers nodded in agreement as the steep roof of the mansion started to crest over the trees.

"Here we go, boys," Logan said, as he rang the doorbell on the front porch. He peered into the dark window overlooking the circular driveway, but there was no answer. Both Logan and one of the officers walked along the east side of the yard and noticed a white van under the carport.

"I think we have the correct residence," Logan whispered under this breath. There was a dim light coming through the kitchen window and he immediately drew his gun. Because the doorknob was locked Logan exposed the handle of his revolver and broke a small square of glass just above the knob. He unlocked the door and slowly walked in the massive kitchen.

The smell of fresh paint was everywhere as he made his way down the main hallway to the spot where Molly Benedict had exposed the hidden room. The entire wall had been completely recovered and painted.

Logan could barely see the floor as the faint orange rays of the sun disappeared through the filthy windows. He noticed a moving shadow from the corner of his eye and ran back to the living room. A door slammed directly behind him as the sound of heavy footsteps echoed throughout the first floor.

Logan opened the door and could hear the torturous sound of heavy panting coming from the basement. He slowly walked down the narrow stairway and noticed Rosenberg lying against a wine rack. Logan ran to his beaten body and placed two fingers on his neck. Rosenberg's eyes opened with terror as he tried to raise his arm to touch Logan's shoulder.

Two hands suddenly appeared on both sides of Logan's head as a bloody steel cable slithered around his neck with reptile-like precision. Logan gasped for air as he clamped onto a set of hairy fingers that were pulling on the cable.

Klaus smiled as he watched Logan helplessly fall to the ground in agonizing pain. "It will all be over soon," Klaus said, as he pulled the cable tighter each time Logan attempted to take a breath.

Logan's face was quickly turning blue as he felt the sides of his windpipe start to collapse under the pressure of the cable. For a moment the pressure relaxed, and Logan struggled to his feet and dug his fingernails into Klaus's hands. But the cable sliced deeper into his soft skin.

Rosenberg noticed an unattended blowtorch lying near the safe with a blue flame searing from the nozzle. He crawled to the torch and gripped the handle with his bound hands while trying to balance his weight. He raised the flame to Klaus's ankle, causing his pant leg to catch on fire. Logan's neck was released as Klaus attempted to roll on the dirt floor to extinguish the spreading flame on his cuff.

Detective Logan fell to the ground in exhaustion as he gripped his bloody neck to gain back a normal breathing pattern. Both Logan and Rosenberg helplessly watched Klaus wail in pain as the flame spread along his clothing. He continued to roll frantically on the basement floor until his body came in contact with an old oil reservoir that once fed a dilapidated furnace. The large container exploded on contact with Klaus's body, and the flames spread to the ceiling and walls of the vacant cellar.

Logan ran to Rosenberg and took the blowtorch from his hand to burn the ropes off his wrists and ankles.

Rosenberg looked at Klaus with horror as the flames consumed the man's body. "Logan, we have to do something."

Logan gasped for air and rubbed his neck in pain.

"This whole place is going to be engulfed in flames. I'm sorry, but I think it's too late to save Klaus."

Molly's screams for help could be heard in the distance as a series of explosions shook the foundation of the house. "Get Molly, I can take care of myself!" Rosenberg yelled over the roar of the flames.

Logan ran down the dark corridor and found Molly lying on the floor completely bound. He took a knife out of his coat and frantically cut the heavy ropes from her bloody arms and legs.

Rosenberg ran to Logan and Molly with a terrified look. "The entire staircase is in flames."

Logan ignored Rosenberg's words. "What about Klaus?"

Rosenberg shook his head. "He didn't make it."

Logan ran back to the cellar to see if there was any chance of escaping through the use of the stairs. Another series of explosions rocked the corridor as he tried to keep his balance against the corridor wall.

Logan slowly made his way back to Rosenberg and Molly as he crawled on the floor to avoid the heavy blanket of smoke that was filling the cramped corridor.

Molly pointed to a ladder on the wall that led to a scuttle hole within the ceiling. Logan climbed up the rickety ladder while holding the end of a small flashlight. The scuttle hole door moved and Logan was engulfed in darkness as his feet disappeared through the small opening. He poked his head back through the hole and motioned for Rosenberg and Molly to follow. Both Molly and Rosenberg frantically climbed the ladder as Logan lit the opening with the light.

Logan reinserted the small door to keep the smoke from pouring in the crawl space as Molly and Rosenberg journeyed ahead to see where the tiny attic opening would lead within the house. Rosenberg started to kick a portion of the wall that was connected to a radiator pipe. The pipe came lose as a blanket of insulation tumbled on Molly, just as Logan caught up from behind.

The gap was small but there was enough room for both Molly and Rosenberg to reach their hands through to tear the wall apart. Logan and Rosenberg both started to kick at the wall as large pieces of plaster tumbled on their heads, making the opening grow larger with every blow. Rosenberg crawled through the opening as he pulled the thick insulation away so Molly and Logan could escape the heat of the crawl space. Logan held up the light and all three of them discovered they had entered the secret room that Molly had discovered just a few days before.

"So that's how those kids got in here," Logan said, as he ran to an outline on the wall where the door once stood. Both he and Rosenberg started to tear down the freshly raised drywall as the intense heat of the fire below gained momentum.

"Please hurry!" Molly yelled, as the smoke rose through the loosely nailed floorboards.

Logan looked back and could see thin clouds of smoke billowing from each crack in the floor. Rosenberg punched his left fist through the heavy drywall and could see one of the officers on the opposite side swinging an axe. Rosenberg stood back as the heavy blade sliced through the beams and drywall with incredible efficiency.

Logan pushed Molly through the makeshift door and Rosenberg soon followed. The main hallway was completely engulfed with smoke as all four of them ran to the kitchen door. The cool lake breeze greeted Molly as she knelt on the front lawn to cough away the smoke.

Logan turned his head towards the lakefront and noticed John in hot pursuit of Cameron Fossberg as both men disappeared in the shadow of the trees.

Cameron's lungs were burning from exhaustion as

he sprinted down the lake path. John's adrenaline was at full peak as he ran in the direction of Cameron's heavy panting. Cameron stumbled over a tree root and fell face first onto the jagged rocks of a retaining wall.

John Benedict tackled Cameron Fossberg with full force and both men fell into the shallow water below. Cameron grabbed a large portion of John's hair and forced his head under the water.

John pulled his head back to the surface and landed a punch in the middle of Cameron's rib cage. Cameron fell into water as he attempted to regain his breath.

John could see Logan and one of the officers running down the lake path. "I'm over here!" John yelled.

Cameron arose out of the water and put John into a headlock. John's body was completely submerged as Cameron struggled to keep his head beneath the surface.

"Let him go!" Logan yelled, as he aimed his revolver at Cameron's head. "*Let him go!*"

Cameron Fossberg released John's head as an officer crawled into the water. John slowly rose to the surface gasping for air as the officer handcuffed

Cameron.

Molly and Rosenberg ran down the cobblestone driveway to escape the heat and smoke of the intense blaze that roared and crackled into the night. They both turned around to take in the awesome sight as the massive structure seemed to be screaming in the agony of its own death.

Rosenberg looked back at the main gate as the wail of sirens bellowed in the distance from an army of fire engines and water tankers. He couldn't help but think of Klaus's body buried in the rubble. His heart was tortured by the fact that he contributed to the death of a human being. Tears began to roll down his face as he watched the mansion's roof fall into an abyss of unforgiving flames.

Molly could see her dad walking up from the lake path and she ran to his arms. They both embraced each other as they watched the once glorious mansion collapse under the fire's wrath in a ball of orange and pitch-black smoke.

*

Two days had passed since the fire, and Rosenberg was spending his last night in the hospital recovering from cracked ribs and a broken collarbone. A nurse was changing bandages on his face when Detective

Logan walked into the room.

"Did they find the safe in all that smoldering rubble?" Rosenberg asked.

Logan wore a big smile. "They sure did. It took some doing, but they finally located it after the smoke died down a bit. The fire department had to hose the thing down with lake water just so they could wrap the winch cable around it."

"I just saw the news on one of the Chicago channels, and they did a pretty descent job of covering the story. Your mug looked pretty good on the tube."

Detective Logan pulled a chair next to the bed and patted Rosenberg's arm. "I couldn't have done it without you."

The elderly reporter leaned his head back as the medication took effect. "It was the least I could do. I didn't want Lauren's death to be swept under the rug just because I was too scared to say anything."

Logan's face became serious. "One of the reasons I came by was to let you know that the district attorney plans to subpoena both you and Molly to testify against Cameron Fossberg."

Rosenberg nodded. "Have they listed the charges against him?"

"Where do I begin? Among the few things on the

top of the list are kidnapping, accessory to murder and arson."

"Arson?" Rosenberg asked, with a surprised look.

Logan took off his coat and leaned against the chair. "The fire department found evidence that Cameron Fossberg helped the fire along. I don't know if he intended to burn the place down all along for the insurance money, or if he panicked when the plan failed."

"What about the two guys with the blow torches?"

Logan started to laugh. "You'll never believe this. We found them hiding in a boat still wearing their welding suits. The only metal they're going to be seeing for a while is jail bars."

Rosenberg couldn't wait any longer to ask the big question. "What about the safe? Did they get it open?"

Logan was slow to answer. "Not yet. The key Lauren sent you definitely belongs to the safe, but no one knows the combination."

"What about Cameron Fossberg? He has to know what it is."

Logan wore a weak smile. "He wouldn't talk if I put a gun to his head. It would just implicate him more if they found out what the safe contained."

Rosenberg was visibly disappointed. "So, what

now?"

Logan sighed heavily. "Different options are being considered, but our police department won't have the safe for very long." Logan leaned back in his chair. "Because it may contain counterfeit printing plates and bills, representatives from the U.S. Treasury Department will be arriving within a few days. It will then be under federal jurisdiction."

"Do you think we'll ever know what's in there?" Rosenberg asked with concern.

"Not unless we can figure out the combination before the feds get their hands on it." Logan reached for his coat and pulled out the lion ring. "I wanted to give this back to you."

Rosenberg slowly opened his hand to take the ring. "Lauren experienced a great deal of suffering for nothing. I wish there was a way to get closure on all of this, but I just don't think it will ever happen."

Logan's lips tightened as he tried to think of something to say. "I firmly believe justice prevails with time."

Rosenberg's eyes were becoming noticeably heavy. "You're probably right, but that's a commodity I'm running low on."

Detective Logan rose to his feet. "I better get

going."

"Thanks for stopping by. I really do appreciate it," Rosenberg said, as he watched Logan exit the room.

He turned the television off and glanced at the ring in his hand. He gently placed the ring on the glass of a hand mirror that was lying on his lap, and slowly closed his eyes.

CHAPTER TEN

Cameron Fossberg was lying on a cot deep in thought when the sound of footsteps echoed against the cold cement floor of the county jail. He rose to his feet and smiled as he noticed his wife Morgan walking to his cell with a guard. The guard opened the heavy iron door and motioned for her to enter the cell.

"You have fifteen minutes," the guard said, as he walked down the cellblock.

Cameron tried to give his wife a hug, but she quickly pushed his arms away. "What have you told them?" Morgan asked with concern.

"Absolutely nothing," Cameron said, as he sat on the end of the cot. "Why did you have to kill that kid and old woman? They weren't going to say anything." He looked at the floor as he rubbed his temples. "I've never met someone who enjoys bloodshed as much as you."

Morgan stood over Cameron and stuck her finger into his chest. "Listen, if it wasn't for your sloppiness, none of this would have happened. You were supposed to take care of the room and that gang of brats. I was just cleaning up another one of your messes."

"Morgan, I don't care if you're Kholton's granddaughter or not, it wasn't supposed to go down like this. You promised there would be no killing. Now my father is dead and the house is nothing more than a pile of rubble. Let's face it, things aren't looking too good."

"Please keep your voice down," Morgan whispered, as she looked down the cellblock.

"I don't care who hears me. You're not the one stuck in this cage. Why don't you get some of your family's high priced lawyers up here and take care of this mess?"

"The wheels are in motion," Morgan said, as she handed Cameron a small paper bag from her purse.

"What's this?" Cameron asked.

"I thought you might want some normal food. I got a few candy bars. It's okay, I checked it through the system."

"Thanks."

Morgan sat next to Cameron on the cot and rubbed his shoulders. "I read in the paper that the district attorney may offer you a deal for your testimony. Is that really true, or is it just the press talking?"

Cameron munched on a candy bar as he enjoyed the back rub. "What am I going to say?" He paused and looked at his wife. "Do you really think I'm going to implicate you?"

Morgan smiled and kissed his cheek. "I trust you, honey." She seemed scared to ask anymore questions. "I just wanted to know what's going on."

Cameron stood up from the cot. "I need to be alone for a while."

Morgan seductively combed her fingers through his hair. "Please don't be mad at me, Cameron. Soon this will all be a memory."

*

John was sitting on the living room couch as he watched Lynn serve Pastor Phil Morse a cup of coffee. "I think these past few days have taken about ten years off my life," John said with a smile.

Phil took a small sip of coffee and placed the mug on the table. "John, would you consider sharing some of your experiences at church?"

John didn't answer right away. Then, "I'll have to think about it."

Molly walked in from the hallway and joined the discussion. "I want to talk about it on Sunday." She paused and looked at Phil. "We can't ignore what happened."

John smiled at Molly. "I'm game, if you're up for it."

"Dad, I'm so sorry all of this happened."

John put his arm around Molly. "I have to believe God had a plan in all of this."

Phil looked at John. "Tell me you mean by that statement."

John took a moment to think about his response. "As an elder it's not easy for me to say this, but when the trials started I felt as if God's protective hand moved away from our home. I know God will never leave our family, but I couldn't understand why all of it was happening."

"Do you think God may have strategically shifted a source of stability in your life?" Phil asked.

John looked confused. "I don't follow what you're saying."

Phil sat up. "Sometimes God will deliberately

place obstacles in our life to get our attention, but there are other times when he may temporarily remove items so we can see the true value of what he has given us."

John scratched the back of his head. "Are you saying that I needed to realize what life may have been like without Molly, in order to truly understand the blessings that God has given me?"

Phil raised a hand to interject a point. "Possibly, but think deeper than just blessings. Who's the source of blessings and hope in life?"

"Jesus," John replied.

Phil smiled. "Exactly. So now you have to return to the two questions we were discussing a minute ago. First, are you using God's tools to navigate around life's obstacles? And secondly, what new level is God raising you to as you readjust the core values of your life because of those obstacles?"

John pondered Phil's questions. "So let me see if I have this straight. You're telling me that in order to truly appreciate the blessings that God has placed in my life, I may need to experience loss in order to gain the blessing back?"

"Not only to gain it back, but to permanently apply God's blessing and promises to your life as well."

John nodded his head as the concept sank in. "I never saw it that way before, but it certainly makes sense. So, in order for a person to truly appreciate peace and stability, they may need to experience the ravages of war."

Phil gave John a high-five. "I think you got it!"

*

Later that night, Rosenberg awoke from a deep sleep as he shifted his body in the hospital bed. He looked down at the mirror on his lap and his mouth dropped wide open.

The mirror's reflection allowed him to see the ring at a reversed angle. The lion's curved tail was comprised of four diamond-studded numeric digits that could only be seen in the opposite direction.

Rosenberg picked up the ring and dialed the phone. "Detective Logan, it's Rosenberg. Call me back as soon as you get this message."

Morgan quietly entered Rosenberg's room wearing a nurse's uniform and gently closed the door. Rosenberg was startled as he hung up the phone. "Can I help you?"

Morgan smiled as she walked to the bed. She noticed the ring in Rosenberg's hand and carefully stroked his fingers. "Give me the ring."

Rosenberg lunged for the nurse pager but Morgan pulled it from his grip and threw it across the room. "I'm not going to ask again. Give me the ring."

*

Detective Logan approached the front desk of the hospital and waited for the attending nurse to get off the phone.

"What can I do for you?" the nurse asked.

Logan showed the nurse his badge. "I was just visiting a friend in room 403 and I forgot my coat."

The nurse was visibly agitated. "Sir, the visiting hours are over."

"I understand that, but my car keys are in the coat. Either I get them or I'll be spending the night in your waiting room."

The nurse waved her hands. "Go ahead, but please make it fast."

Logan walked down the long hospital corridor and opened the door to Rosenberg's room. Logan was startled to see a nurse smothering Rosenberg's face with a pillow.

"Freeze!" Logan yelled, as he drew his gun.

Morgan released her hands from the pillow and looked at Logan. "You wouldn't dare shoot a woman."

Logan cocked the revolver and lifted the muzzle at eye level. “Do you want to find out?”

Morgan smiled as she slowly put her hands behind her back. “So, you’re the famous Detective Logan that everyone is talking about.”

“And who might you be?” Logan asked.

Rosenberg’s face appeared behind the pillow as Logan retrieved his handcuffs. “Logan, she’s got a gun!” Rosenberg yelled.

Morgan pulled out a pistol from behind her back and pointed it at Rosenberg’s head. “What’s it going to be?”

Logan kept his gun pointed at Morgan’s face. “What do you want?”

Morgan smiled as she looked at Logan. “I want the ring, and for you to forget I was ever here.”

Logan felt confused by her answer. “You never answered my first question.”

“I know, because it’s none of your concern who I am,” Morgan said, as she took the ring from Rosenberg’s hand.

Morgan turned to look at Rosenberg, and Logan slapped the gun out of her hand. Morgan dove to the floor to get the gun but Logan grabbed her shoulder and threw her against the wall. He pinned her arms together and put the handcuffs tightly around her wrists. "Let's go, sister. I've had enough excitement for one night."

*

Logan arrived at the station extra early the next morning to catch up on some paperwork. He leaned back in his chair and looked around the office room as he took a long sip of coffee. A few officers returning from the night shift walked down the hallway towards the locker rooms as the janitor finished polishing the floors.

One of the officers approached Logan from behind and tapped his shoulder. "Tough break on that Black Point informant."

Logan put his coffee down. "What are you talking about?"

The officer leaned against Logan's desk. "Didn't you hear?"

"Hear what?" Logan snapped.

"Cameron Fossberg was found dead in his cell during role call this morning." The officer paused as he watched Logan's face turn to a pale white. "They think he was poisoned."

"What!" Logan slammed both hands on top of his desk.

"One of the jail guards said his wife visited him last night. The body was taken to the county corner this morning for a full autopsy," the officer explained. "Didn't anyone tell you? It's been on the scanners for at least an hour."

Logan got up from his chair and ran down the hallway. He burst through a set of doors that lead to some holding cells in the back of the station. "Guard, open the door," Logan said, as he glared at Morgan.

Morgan sat up in the cot with a smile on her face. "Detective Logan, what a nice surprise."

Logan walked in the cell and locked the door. "You killed him, didn't you?"

"What are you talking about?"

"Your husband. That's what I'm talking about."

"Sometimes you have to cut your losses. Unfortunately for you, there's no way to prove anything."

Logan heard his name being paged over the public address system. "I'll be back."

"I'll be waiting for you," Morgan said with a laugh, as she watched the officer escort Logan out of the cell.

Logan walked back to his desk and saw Rosenberg waiting for him. "They let you out of hospital already?"

Rosenberg could tell that Logan wasn't himself. "What's the matter?"

"Cameron Fossberg was killed last night."

"But how?" Rosenberg inquired. "He was in jail."

"I can't prove it, but I know his wife Morgan was behind it."

Rosenberg didn't want to change the subject but he was on a mission to open the safe. "What do you think? Can we open it?"

Logan's was still frustrated. "Okay, but let's make it fast. An FBI agent is supposed to be showing up this morning."

Logan and Rosenberg walked to the far corner of the evidence room where the safe was sitting on a large wooden pallet. Logan entered the key into the slot as Rosenberg read the numbers from the lion ring. Rosenberg's shaky hands pulled the rusted handle and the heavy safe door slowly squeaked open.

"Can you believe it?" Rosenberg asked, as he stared at the safe.

Logan raised his eyebrows. "It's true. There really was a counterfeit conspiracy."

Rosenberg carefully took out a stack of bills that were neatly wrapped with paper straps that bore the Nazi seal. "This is like a movie," he said as he studied the pile of bills.

Logan pointed at the date on one of the bills. "This stuff has been in here for nearly forty years."

"Forty-five to be exact," a voice said from behind.

Logan and Rosenberg turned around with startled looks on their faces.

A man in a black business suit approached Logan and Rosenberg, and shook both their hands. "I'm Agent Ross, and you're handling the property of the United States Government," Ross said, as he held up an FBI badge.

Logan rose to his feet. "Nice to meet you . . . I'm sorry, I didn't get your first name."

"It's Agent Ross. And you are?"

"I'm Detective Logan and this is J.R. Rosenberg."

"Detective Logan, I need you to close this safe immediately and release the prisoner as well."

"What prisoner?" Logan asked.

Agent Ross handed Logan some papers. "The Black Point investigation is now a federal concern and is out of your jurisdiction."

Logan studied the papers as Agent Ross took out a pen. "I'm sorry to inform you that Cameron Fossberg died last night."

Agent Ross was visibly getting irritated. "That's

not the prisoner I'm talking about."

"Then who are you talking about?" Logan asked.

"Are you not holding a Mrs. Morgan Fossberg for questioning?"

"How did you know that?"

"Detective Logan, the FBI appreciates your work on this case, but I can't share information relating to this investigation. If you would be so kind as to sign these papers, my men will be transporting the safe and the prisoner."

Logan refused to look at the papers and placed them on top of the safe. "Are you telling me that you knew Morgan Fossberg was somehow involved with all of this from the start?"

"Let's just say that we have been monitoring the situation for some time now. The activities of the Fossbergs have not been a secret at the bureau."

"But you're taking the only suspect that we have left in our murder case," Logan said with a commanding tone.

"I'm sorry, Detective, but the federal case that we have against Mrs. Fossberg has higher priority."

Logan's face was turning visibly red. "Agent Ross, are you telling me that a safe full of counterfeit money is more important than the lives of four people?"

Mayor Troy Becker walked into the room with the district attorney by his side. "I'm sorry, Frank, but we don't have any authority to hold the safe or the prisoner," Becker said.

"How can this be?" Logan demanded. "We have four dead people, a burned down mansion and a beat up old safe full of money that surfaced in my murder investigation. And now you're telling me that because this guy has a federal badge he can just take it all away because he says so? What country are we living in?"

Vicki Stratton, the district attorney, was looking irritated with Logan's remarks. Stratton was a woman in her late fifties. Despite the fact that she and Detective Logan had worked together on many cases in the past, it was common knowledge that there was no lost love between the two of them.

"Frank, I don't like this anymore than you do, but we can't fight the federal government on this." Stratton scratched her forehead. "We need to get some binding evidence linking Morgan Fossberg to those murders. I know about the incident with Mr. Rosenberg in the hospital but it's not enough to hold her in comparison to a federal case. As far as we know the two main suspects are Klaus and Cameron Fossberg, and they're both dead."

Logan pointed his finger at Stratton. "Vicki, you knew that Cameron Fossberg was found dead in his cell last night?" Logan felt shocked that Stratton knew about Cameron's death before he did. "How about the fact that Morgan was the last known person to see him? That doesn't mean anything to you?"

Stratton looked at Ross. "Did you know about that?"

"We had knowledge of this incident, but finding any conclusive evidence that she was directly linked could be like finding a needle in a hay stack," Ross said with a grin. "I'll tell you what, if you find any evidence that directly links her to Cameron Fossberg's death, I'll give you any pertinent information that could help your case. The bureau has spent the last ten months following the Fossbergs and we're not about to see all our efforts float away. There's too much at stake."

Stratton signed the release papers as Ross placed the safe key into an evidence bag. "I really do appreciate your work on this case, but you have to understand that this investigation reaches far beyond Williams Bay," Ross said, as he sealed the bag.

Logan and Rosenberg watched as the safe was carted down to a van bearing federal plates. Ross and two other special agents escorted Morgan Fossberg to the back of the van as her shackles dragged clumsily on the hot parking lot pavement.

Agent Ross looked at Logan and Rosenberg with a smile. “Thanks for your help.”

Logan and Rosenberg watched the van gradually disappear from site as it sped down the highway towards the interstate.

“Something just doesn’t add up,” Logan said as he noticed Stratton and Becker looking down from the station’s main entryway.

CONCLUSION

A week had passed since the Black Point investigation ended, and Detective Logan was leaning over his desk attempting to finish case reports before the weekend. Thoughts about the Black Point case were still fresh in his mind as he pondered the events of the past three weeks. Logan still hadn't heard from the feds, and something was telling him that he probably never would.

He picked up a thick file folder near the middle of his desk and wrote *Black Point* on a label. With frustration he slowly opened the folder and paged through all the reports, photos and notes from the case.

"Detective Logan, call on line one. Detective Logan, call on line one," the public address speaker blared throughout the station.

Logan reluctantly picked up the phone. “Logan here.”

His cheeks became hollow as he listened to the voice on the other end. “I’ll be right there.”

*

Logan’s car slowly entered the Button’s Bay Recreational Park on the east shore of Lake Geneva, as forensic officers took snap shots of a dead body lying on the edge of a wooded area of the grounds.

A uniformed officer approached Logan while he exited his car. “Detective, I’m sorry to call you down here, but I think you might be interested in seeing this.”

The stench emanating from the corpse saturated the crime scene as Logan uncovered the victim. His eyes stared at the badly decayed face of a woman whose forehead bore the unmistakable imprint of the Black Point lion. “Do our forensic boys have any idea how long the body has been here?” Logan asked, as he studied the deep strangulation lines on the victim’s neck.

“Five or six days. They should be able to track down a name from the dental records,” the officer replied, as he watched Logan kneel over the body.

Logan immediately recognized the unusual

cheekbones and nose of the victim. "I know who it is," he said softly as he re-covered the victim's face.

"Who is it?" the officer asked.

Logan stood up and looked at the cloudless sky. "Her name is Morgan Fossberg."

The officer raised his eyebrows. "Morgan Fossberg? Who's she?"

Logan ignored the question as he walked back to his car. "Those weren't federal agents," he whispered to himself in disbelief.

Logan rubbed his temples as he walked to the edge of the beach and glared at the charred rubble of the Black Point property looming in the far distance across the lake. "Maybe Rosenberg was right," he said to himself. "There may never be closure with the secrets of Black Point."